Any Given Power

ANY
GIVEN
POWER

To Katherine!
god writing

Alissa York

ARBEITER RING PUBLISHING • WINNIPEG

Arbeiter Ring Publishing
2-91 Albert Street
Winnipeg, Manitoba
Canada R3B 1G5
arbeiter@tao.ca
http://www.tao.ca/~arbeiter/

Printed in Canada by the workers at Transcontinental Printing

Cover by Doowah Design

Author photo by Clive Holden

Of these stories, "The Back of the Bear's Mouth" was first published in *Prairie Fire*, "Those Who Trespass" in *PRISM International*, "A Real Present" in *eye wuz here* (Douglas & McIntyre), and "Thank Christ it was Winter" in *The New Quarterly*.

With assistance of the Manitoba Arts Council/Conseil des Arts du Manitoba.

MANITOBA ARTS COUNCIL   Arts   CONSEIL DES ARTS DU MANITOBA

Canadian Cataloguing in Publication Data

York, Alissa.

  Any given power

  ISBN 1-894037-09-X

1. Title.

PS8597.O46A658 1999   C813'.54   C99-920158-1
PR9199.3.Y53A658 1999

for Clive

evolution ... **1** gradual development, esp. from a simple to a more complex form ... **3** the appearance or presentation of events etc. in due succession (*the evolution of the plot*) ... **6** an opening out. **7** the unfolding of a curve. **8** the extraction of a root from any given power.

— *The Oxford Concise Dictionary*

CONTENTS

S A D   B A S T A R D S

IT MIGHT'VE BEEN the war that did it. He only caught about three weeks of action before his leg got blown off, but it was enough, my mother always said, it was enough. He didn't have to work after that and maybe that made it worse — he wasn't much use to himself or anybody else without a job. Oh he got the pension alright. And me and Danny made up for whatever that didn't cover. We helped out at the lumber yard on Saturdays and after school, and never even thought about keeping the money. Sure we skinned a little off the top now and then. We were good sons, but we weren't the Lord Jesus himself.

It might've been the work. She said he kept his hand in around the house at first. Splitting kindling sitting down on a fold-out stool, or else hopping around the yard, throwing scratch to the chickens. Sometimes he even went hunting. He'd go out with Uncle Ray and Gerry Fines, and they'd go off and leave him in some covered spot, and he'd hide his crutches in the brush and lie down in the leaf mould and the mushrooms and wait. He bagged stuff too. A couple of rabbits or a grouse. One time even a buck. The rack was up on the wall, but whenever me or Danny tried to get him to tell us about it he just sunk down deeper in his chair. 'I shot a buck,' he'd say. 'You can see that, can't you?'

'Yah but tell us. Where were ya? When'd ya spot it? Was it alone?'

Then silence. Or else, 'You Dan, change that channel. I can't watch these faggots.' Or the clink of his ring finger on the glass, and him holding it out to get filled.

'What happened?' I asked her. 'Why'd he stop — doing everything?'

'Nothing happened,' she said after a minute. 'What happened was he stopped.'

That's what got me thinking. It was his birthday coming up. He was coming on to fifty, older than her. They never even had us boys until after he came back, so he was still doing that for a while too, I guess. It would've been hard I suppose, embarrassing even, with just the one leg. Now he just slept in that chair, flipped up the footrest and kicked back, letting his mouth drop open.

Anyway, I got to thinking about hunting. For his fiftieth — for a surprise — me and Danny could take him hunting. It was November, with the leaves all turned and deer in season. Then it came to me like a picture. The cabin at Dawkins Lake. Uncle Ray was dead some years, but there was no road access, so it wasn't likely anybody would've found the place, let alone taken it over. We'd been there a few times as kids. There was no hunting on those summer trips, mostly just the two of us running around like wild Indians and the men playing cards inside.

It'd be a mess by now. The mice would've got at any dry goods or lard or blankets left in the place, but so what, we'd just take along whatever we needed. Bacon and bread and coffee and a couple of bottles. There'd be firewood enough.

I told Danny when we were down at the yard, the two of us unloading a pallet of cinder blocks. I had to whip him into the spirit of the thing.

'He'd never go,' is what he said at first.

'He will if we do it right,' I told him, 'take care of everything. Alls he has to do is get in the car. Well?' I said. 'C'mon Danny.' There was something kind of desperate in the way I said it. 'He's gotta be dyin to get out.'

He was holding a block in each hand and he just stood there with his shoulders straining. Then he nodded. 'Alright,' he said, 'maybe you got somethin there.'

We never let on. We cleaned the rifles and aired out the sleeping bags in the shed, and Danny took care of whatever we needed foodwise, so we didn't even need to tell her. Oh she could smell something was up alright.

'What're you boys doing out there?' she called out more than once. 'I got pie and coffee here. Your father's waiting.'

'Coming Ma'am,' was all we said. We covered everything over with tarps, and God knows if she ever set foot in that dingy shed anyways. That was the kind of dust and grime she didn't want to know about, where the dirt was part of what held things together. You couldn't see her in there. She was always somewhere warm and clean — in the kitchen or by the fire — looking over the tops of her glasses, reading some magazine she'd got given to her, or cutting half-moons or stars to sew into her latest quilt. Those glasses were for an older woman. Same as the dresses she wore and the way she twisted her hair up tight. But a lot of women were like that then — married with kids was married with kids. I guess she was something fine when they met. There was that old picture, chestnut curls down her back and the lips coloured in pink. You could tell anyway, just looking at her while she stirred a pot. Her hands were gone, red and puffy with the nails bitten down, but in that picture they were like little birds. One of them flying white through her hair.

She looked up scared when I told him. It was supper on his birthday eve. He was at the head and me on his right, the oldest. Danny to his left and her at the other end, the tail I guess, the end nearest the stove so she could get up and down.

'Guess what?' I said to him, and for a long time it looked like he was going to go right on eating.

'Yah,' said Danny, 'guess.'

He looked up from the potatoes he was shovelling in. He didn't say, 'What?' He wasn't the kind to answer *guess what?* with *what?* He just stared. First at me, then at Danny. Then one of his eyebrows crawled up, the one with the scar cutting through.

She'd gone all quiet down the tail end. Laid her fork down and maybe even left off breathing.

'Well,' I started in. My voice cracked a little, like I thought it was over and done with doing. 'Well.'

'That's a hole in the ground son,' he said, about the closest he ever came to a joke.

'Yah. Well. Me and Danny. Seeing as it's your birthday tomorrow, your fiftieth and all. Well. We thought you might like to go hunting. Maybe bag us a deer.'

Danny came in then, kind of excited, talking fast. 'We got everything ready. We got it all planned. We'll go out to Uncle Ray's old place. We got everything ready already.' He looked at me for a second and I nodded. 'Alls you gotta do is get in the car.'

Then Danny went quiet. We were all quiet and all of a sudden I felt guilty — bad — like me and Danny just told them we were leaving, or one of us'd got some girl pregnant, or something else bad like that.

She was the first one to speak. 'That's nice boys. That's real nice. I'm sure your father appreciates it. I'm sure he does. Only he might not feel up to a trip like that, and that's the thing. He might —'

'Who says?' The old man cut a fatty piece off his chop and started grinding on it. 'Who says I don't feel up to it?'

She fell quiet.

'Okay,' I said. 'So what if we get going around nine? That way we can get out there and set up and maybe have something to eat before dusk.'

I didn't expect him to answer me but he did.

'O nine hundred,' he said. And then he saluted.

I took the wheel and he got in beside me. Danny tied the trunk down with the crutches sticking out and then piled into the back.

The old man narrowed his eyes out the windshield, to where the nose of the boat came down like a beak, tied to the bumper with a length of yellow rope. 'You sure she's tied on good?'

'Yessir,' I said.

'Yessir,' said Danny.

I was backing out of the drive when I looked up and saw her smiling down at us from the porch. Smiling and twisting the dishrag in her hands. I hit the horn a couple of times, then pulled us out onto the road.

It was smooth enough getting there. Danny did most of the talking, him the joker with me playing the straight man, handing him the lines.

'Looks like the Hendersons finally got rid of that heap,' I said, and Danny said, 'Yah, they'll never get rid of those girls though. You think you know ugly when you spot one of them girls, but that's just 'til the other one shows up.'

The old man didn't say much, but I was watching him in the corner of my eye. Sometimes he grinned a little at whatever Danny was saying. And when we turned onto the dirt track that led down to the lake, he pointed at a flash of blue in the trees and said, 'Steller's jay.'

The lake was calm. Carrying the boat down to the dock, me and Danny didn't have to speak. We'd lifted so many things together, carried so much stuff from here to there between us that we acted like one body, him matching my backward-walking pace just right, never pushing and making me stumble, never hanging back so I had to yank or strain. We got the boat into the water and the Evinrude down with the old man standing teetery on the edge of the dock, slumped on his crutches looking out.

'Looks like a good day for it huh?' I said to him, and he did me the favour of grunting.

We got all the gear stowed in tight and the rifles lying long and shiny alongside the oars and then he wouldn't take any help getting in. He eased the crutches out beside him, bracing them dockboard by dockboard, until he was down low enough to slip them out from under his arms and sit down hard. He pulled the boat in close with his foot, then reached down with his arms and kind of dragged himself in, his stump catching on the gunnel for a few seconds, making him struggle so he almost turned the boat tits up. Almost. Then he was in. Sitting pretty at the tiller. Me and Danny climbed in side by side in the middle seat like kids, and he started her up on the third pull, and we were away.

The water was green. Once or twice you could make out the flash of a trout not too far down, and Danny said, 'Jeez if my hand was a net I coulda got that one.'

Everything seemed peaceful. I looked Danny in the eye, as if to say, *See, he's happy*, and Danny trailed his fingers over the side and gave me a smile.

Then the loon started up. It let loose over and over, and when I happened to look back at the old man the tiller was slack in his hand and we were way off course. He was steering us to the cliffs on the far shore, far from the sandy inlet where we were meant to land. He caught me looking and the loon screamed and he shook his head hard, like there was water in his ears. Then he yanked on the tiller and brought the boat back in line.

We were headed along fine then. The inlet was growing up in size, the same colour and curve as the inside of somebody's hand. The lake was rippling, lit up and glinting like the scales on a giant green fish.

That's when he did it. I don't know how the hell he slid the rifle out from beside my leg without me or Danny catching on. I'll never know how he did that. Maybe we were just too zeroed in on that inlet. Or maybe that howling loon was all we had room for in our ears, but the fact was he got hold of it and slid the bolt back and shot over the side at a fish.

'What the?!' Danny was ducked down beside me, and then I found I was ducked down too, something your body does without you I guess, when a gun goes off that close by.

'Jesus,' I said, and Danny said, 'Christ Almighty.'

The tiller was loose. We were headed nowhere fast, slowed down to idle, turning a tight circle on the spot. I looked around the lake. Nobody. The shot was still echoing, coming back at us from the ring of trees. He was sighting along the barrel again, only this time he had the muzzle stuck down in the water.

'Jesus Sir,' I said, 'you're gonna bust your barrel!'

Danny was still hunkered down beside me, looking back at him big-eyed like a dog or a kid.

'Sir,' I said again, 'you know you can't shoot fish.'

'Little fucker,' he said under his breath. I was starting to feel sick then, watching the lake go round and round.

'Sir,' I said, talking the way the doctor talks when he's about to give you a shot, 'you gotta put the gun down. You gotta take the tiller. You gotta get us to shore.'

The loon was quiet now. It shut up the second the rifle went off.

'Hnnn?' One of his eyes left off sighting and lifted over to me. 'Hnn?'

'You can't shoot fish Sir. You'd catch hell if anybody saw. We'd all catch hell.' It hit me then how strange it was to be trying to tell somebody something, when they're the one who taught you that thing in the first place.

He was looking at me like he just woke up. Then he shook his head again, but really it was more like his head shook on its own. He pulled the barrel up out of the water and slid the rifle back in along-side me, pushing the butt with his boot. I reached down and thumbed on the safety. He wouldn't look at me then. He took the tiller in both hands and pulled us round, fixed his sights on the inlet and opened her up.

He brought us in fine after that. Just about perfect. He cut the engine just right and tilted it up out of the water, and me and Danny jumped over the side and sent the minnows flying. We pulled the tail-end round and held steady while he struggled out, first sinking the tips of his crutches into the knee-high water, then hauling himself up, leaning into them and pulling his leg up like a spring, swinging out and over and landing with his boot on the hard-packed sand. You couldn't believe it when he didn't fall. One after the other, he yanked the crutches out from behind him, then started making his way up the beach toward the overgrown mouth of the trail. Me and Danny hauled the boat up and unloaded the gear and flipped her over on the sand.

'What the hell,' Danny said to me, 'what the hell was all that?'

I was loading the bigger of the two packs onto my back. 'Yah,' I said. But I was the oldest, even if only by a year. *The eldest*, she always said when she was trying to teach me what that meant, how I had to look out for Danny, how I had to be the one to keep an even keel. 'He just forgot is all. Forgot where he was for a second, I guess.'

Danny had his pack on now, the faded green one with all the pockets. Somehow I'd never thought about it before, but that pack must've belonged to the old man in the war. Maybe he kept hand grenades in those pockets. Crawling on his belly through the mud and the blackness and the blood.

He was up where the sand gave way to salal and scrubby trees. He looked back at us over his hunched up shoulder and beckoned, his hand moving short and sharp, like it was urgent.

'C'mon,' I said, 'we'd be a couple of sad bastards if a cripple could lose us in the bush.'

I'd remembered the cabin being closer. Like snapshots — there's the beach, then there's the cabin. In actual fact it took about an hour to get there. It would've taken me and Danny half that time, even with those heavy packs, but the old man led the way, cursing the trip roots and pushing through with his head down, letting the overgrown switches snap back.

He was muttering. I couldn't make out what he was saying, and Danny probably couldn't even hear from where he was bringing up the rear, but he was muttering alright. The good feeling I'd got going in the car and on the peaceful first half of the lake was pretty much gone.

The cabin looked like hell. We came out into what used to be the clearing and there it was — about half the size I remembered, with eaten-through plastic on the windows and the outhouse rotted down into the bush out back. Like one of those shacks gold-panners go nuts in. The four walls closing in.

He swung up on his crutches and kicked open the door. 'Home sweet home,' he said.

Inside was worse. Rats or mice had torn half the stuffing out of the old car seat sofa, and there were rye bottles lined up sticky on every cupboard and shelf, along the walls even, with bugs drowned and pickled in the bottoms and spider webs strung out between.

'Looks like somebody's been partying.' Danny tried out a grin, but in the half-light of that place it just made him look creepy. We both knew the bottles weren't from any time recent. Somehow you don't pay attention when you're a kid. It hit me that they must've been drinking that whole time — him and Gerry Fines and Uncle Ray — the whole time we were out making snares in the woods, or laying in the tent outside, me scaring the shit out of Danny, saying, 'D'ya hear that? It's a big mother, whatever it is.'

But that's what goes on, I guess. It's nothing so different. It's just what men do when they're out hunting or fishing. Anywhere there's no woman to look at them sideways.

Danny was trying to be cheerful. 'Jeez,' he said, 'I'm starvin. Where's that bacon anyways?' He started rifling through both packs, making a production out of it, clanking the cast iron pan and the forks and the three tin cups. 'You wanna start a fire?' he said to me, and I took his lead.

'Yah,' I said, 'sounds good.'

We skirted round him. There wasn't much choice — he was standing stock still in the middle of the room, like a tree grown up through the floor.

There was still some kindling and a few good pieces out in the lean-to. Maybe split by him, sitting on a stump and swinging the hatchet, getting me and Danny to gather the pieces in a pile.

The spiders had a city in there now. A big one jumped out from the bark on a knotty piece and made a break for it up my arm, headed for my rolled-up sleeve. It was all I could do not to scream like a woman. I dropped the wood and shook it off, black legs pulled in for the fall, then spread out and scuttling, too fast for the heel of my boot.

I got the fire blazing and by then the old man'd sat down on a hard-backed chair. Danny cooked the bacon and bread together in the pan, and got a can of water boiling for coffee. I sat down on the car sofa and watched.

The old man was looking into the stove. Rubbing his stump with the flat of his hand and staring past the door grate into the flames. I could tell by the way he picked up his cup and held it out, it wasn't coffee he wanted. It was the same way he held out his glass at home — like a blind man on the street, no expression on his face, not a word, and her filling it for him every time.

I fished out a bottle. I poured him out two fingers, but he tapped the tin lip of the cup against the bottle neck, so I poured out a couple more. Me and Danny had coffee. Danny made a move for the bottle but I shook my head ever so gently no. Not that we hadn't drank with him before. She never liked it because we weren't yet legal, but he'd get us loaded every now and then, Christmas or Easter or sometimes just Sunday dinner. It wasn't much fun, not while we were stuck in the house with him getting quieter instead of louder like us. How could booze do that — make the blood run to bursting in me and Danny while it drained every drop out of him? It would end up with him telling us to shut up, and her saying, 'Why don't you boys take a walk, maybe see what's going on in town. I don't want you taking the car, mind. You take a walk.'

The two of us whooping through the woods like a couple of ape men, or else knocking together down the deserted main street, talking about what we'd do to what girl if we got hold of her. 'Give 'er

the two-finger salute. Give 'er a corn dog and a ride at the fair.'
Killing ourselves laughing. Falling down laughing in the street.

We'd drank with the old man plenty of times, but somehow, out
there in the boondocks, it didn't look like such a hot idea.

When we were done with the food I wiped my hands on my
jeans and stood up. 'Wellsir,' I said, 'whaddaya say we get out there.
Head down to that poplar break maybe. Deer won't be movin for a
while yet, but there's bound to be one or two of 'em bedded down.'

'Hnnn,' he said.

'Danny boy,' I said, 'you wanna get them rifles together?'

'Sure,' said Danny, and he went over by the door and looked
busy.

'Sir,' I said, 'you 'bout set?'

'Hnn,' he said again, and then he held out his cup.

I took a chance. I didn't reach for the bottle, at least not right
away. 'I thought we might get going,' I said. 'You know, get out
there.'

He was looking into the cup, looking hard, like he might've
been trying to fill it by will. Then he shook it. Lifted it up in my face
and shook it like a fist.

That's when I knew he wasn't going to hunt after all. I wanted to
say *Why?* To scream it really, *Why in hell did you let us bring you here
then? Me and Danny busting our asses, getting everything just right and
now look — all you want to do is sit on your can and stare and drink. Just
like at home, you sonofabitch cripple*, I wanted to scream, but Danny was
behind me by the door, and I had to keep an even keel, and anyway,
I didn't have the guts. I filled his cup. As near to the top as I could
without running over. Then I set the bottle down where he could
reach it on the floor.

'Well,' I said. 'That's about where we'll get started, the poplar
break — if you wanna come along later on.'

Danny handed me my rifle. It made me nervous somehow,
leaving the old man there with his .303 cleaned and loaded. Not
like I could take it with me. It was the last thing I caught sight of,

leaned up gleaming at me as I shut the slat door.

I felt a bit better once the shack was out of sight. I was letting Danny take the lead, like giving a kid a piece of candy when he's had a scare, or walked in on something he's too young to see.

'You think,' he said to me, not looking back, 'you think he's — ?'

'I don't think nothin.' I cut him off, and for a second I heard myself sounding like the old man, my voice dropping out of me like a rock. Danny didn't say much after that, just marched on up ahead of me, with that pack in my face and me falling in step, the two of us holding our rifles crossways on our chests.

Then we were into the poplars. Grey-green slippery trunks, not one of them thicker than I could close my hands round. The leaves overhead and underfoot, yellow and yellow and more yellow. All of a sudden I remembered running there — Danny and me — not chasing each other or anything, just running because we had to, cupping the smooth trunks in our hands, swinging. I remembered it like our feet skimmed over the ground, like we were swooping more than running, swinging and swooping, flying through the trees.

Danny cupped his hand round a tree trunk then, and I knew the same memory was moving in his head. Then I felt lucky. *I'm a lucky sonofabitch*, I thought to myself there in the November light, and this feeling ran down through my chest and into my belly, like a glass of warm sugared milk.

'I'm gonna set up here,' I said. 'Take cover and wait for them deer to get movin.'

'Okay,' said Danny. 'I'll go on a ways.'

I watched him move away from me, turtle-shaped in between the trees. Then I found some brush, crawled under it and settled in.

A funny thing happens when you sit still in the woods. Everything goes quiet. It seems like all the sound has been sucked out of the air, and then bit by bit you can really hear, and if you wait long enough, you can even see.

I pretty much forgot I was there to hunt. I watched a couple of red squirrels chase and fight and ride the high thin branches up and down. A marten eased by a few feet from my boots, with its belly low to the ground and a shrew still kicking in its teeth. A woodpecker landed on the closest tree. It was only a little one, but I could feel it pecking, shaking the tree, and the tree roots shaking the ground, and up through the ground into me.

I thought about heading down after Danny, since dusk was coming up and no deer seemed to be moving my way, but the truth was I felt alright where I was. That warm milk feeling had spread out all through me. I laid my rifle down and drifted into a sitting-up sleep.

The doe was there when I woke up. Her face was so close and the way she was looking right at me, I had to wonder if I was dreaming. There wasn't much light. I reached out ever so slowly for the gun, but the barrel was so cold it stung my fingers. I couldn't bring myself to pick it up. She was watching me. Her soft black nose and those eyes and me tucked up in the bush — somehow not stiff like I should've been, but warm and loose, like that feeling right after you come off.

That's when it happened. A shot, then another, then another, spaced out even, not far, maybe a mile. The help signal. *Danny.* The deer was gone. Disappeared. *Danny, Jesus.* I grabbed hold of my rifle, struggled up out of the bush and started running. Now the trees were no game. Darker and darker, they were a maze, a nightmare, me crashing through them like a crazy man, thinking, *Where is he where is he, which way to the shots,* and then suddenly I knew. It came to me like a picture — not like a photograph, more like a painting, with the colours more real than you see them, and the light like you feel it inside. He was in the old spruce grove we used to call the Church. That heavy sap smell and the cool and the sun turning stained-glass colours through the trees. He was there. I knew it. And then I could hear him, the high thin howl of a puppy, then deeper, loud as a full-grown hound. *It's bad,* I said over and over in my head, running, 'Oh Jesus,' I said out loud, 'it's bad.'

He was bent over on his side at the foot of the oldest tree in the Church.

'Danny!' I screamed and he screamed back at me. Then I saw it. The trap closed tight around his leg and the leg bent the wrong way and the bone sticking out through the skin in two places, like teeth in the teeth of the trap. Not just any trap. A huge old leg-hold, so rusty the metal was lifting up in bubbles. I was down on my knees beside him, talking in her voice now, straining against the spring, saying, 'Danny, Danny boy, I'm here now, hold still now Danny, hold still.'

The rust hadn't weakened it one bit — if anything it was worse, the metal grinding together and sticking now it was sprung. Danny had no strength to help me. It was night now, but there was a hunter's moon rising, and I could see the ground around him was dark and spongy with blood. I couldn't lift him. Even if I could get the drag's anchor unwound from the tree's roots, the weight of the trap would tear his leg clean off. The weight of it would kill him for sure.

'Danny,' I said. He was breathing fast, his eyes rolling back white with the pain. 'I gotta go get him. We'll be back before you know it, Danny. Hold on.'

Then back through the trees, moonlight now, the ghost trunks gleaming, me stumbling and running, dropping my rifle and leaving it, running, then the path, low brush and the ember light of the shack. I broke in on him passed out in his chair. I had the strength of two men then, too late, lifting and shaking him. 'Wake up for Chrissakes! Wake up you bastard, you bastard!' And my face was wet and running down my neck, so I must've been crying.

'It's Danny!' I screamed. He opened his eyes. 'Danny's leg!' I screamed in his face. 'Bear trap! Trap!'

He fell more than once on the way. I swung the flashlight round and he was on his hands and knee, or another time bent sideways over a rock.

'You hurt yourself now and I'll kill you,' I said through my teeth. 'I'll kill you,' I said quietly, and I ran back and picked up his crutches and helped him get up. He reeked. *I'll never take another drink*, I thought, *so help me, I'll never, ever take another drink.*

At first I thought Danny was dead. In the flashlight beam he was the colour of the shelf fungus growing out of the tree behind him. His hands were turned palm-up on the ground. The old man threw down his crutches and fell down beside him, pulled a small round mirror out of his coat pocket and held it up to Danny's mouth. I'll never get over that, that mirror like a tiny lake in his hand. What the hell was he doing with a mirror? Did he look at himself in it? Take it out to check if he was still there?

'Hold that light steady,' he said, and there was steam on the mirror, not much steam, but enough. 'C'mon,' he told me, 'you get hold of that half.'

He was strong. I can't say how, but he was strong as a bull. We had that trap open in a few seconds, and Danny's leg free and bleeding freely on the ground. The old man had his coat off. He was pulling his shirt off and tearing it into strips.

'Get a couple of branches,' he said, not looking up, 'straight ones, for a splint.'

When I got back with the branches, he said, 'Hold him fast, under his arms there, lock your fingers over his chest.'

He crawled round to Danny's foot and pulled his knife from its sheath and cut the boot away. Then he took the bloody sock foot in his hands and yanked. The sharp ends of the bone slipped back inside Danny's leg. Danny screamed. His eyes fluttered blue for a second then fell shut, and I moved my hand down to his wrist and felt until I found a pulse. The old man was tying a strip tight above where it was bleeding, then more strips to hold his undershirt on over the wound. He had his own leg slid under Danny's to hold it up. Then he padded it with his coat, showed me how to hold the branches and tied them alongside the leg. He was naked from the waist up. I went to give him my coat but he was already up on his crutches. 'Gimme the flashlight,' he said, 'you pick him up.'

I bent to lift Danny over my shoulder, and he said, 'No, like a woman. Pick him up like a woman.'

It was a hell of a long way, Danny coming to now and then and howling and twisting in my arms and me panting, 'It's okay Danny, you're okay Danny, you're okay.' Following the old man's bare back through the trees, him taking those crutches like a pole-vaulter, the flashlight swinging up and down in his mouth, and me with that weight barely able to keep up.

He let me take the tiller. We had Danny laid out long over the seats, with his head in my lap and the old man facing me, holding the splint steady on his stump. That was something alright — his scrawny white chest in the moonlight. Him cradling that leg in his hands.

THOSE WHO TRESPASS

It was the size of an apple. That's what the doctor told me, so that's how I saw it in my head — a dark red delicious, all shiny and perfect, cut out of my guts.

You think you'd know it if something was swelling up that big where it didn't belong, but somehow I never felt a thing. Not until that cyst was good and ripe. It was the same day my dad dropped the bomb. Stared down at his boots and mumbled how we were moving out, just me and him, and Maureen wasn't coming along.

'It's been building a long time Robin,' was how he explained it.

Maureen was in the armchair, with mascara branching out in her crow's feet and the rosary balled up in her fist. 'You don't have to go Robin,' she told me, 'you know you can stay here with me.' But I couldn't take the hand she held out. I kept close by my dad, the two of us standing and Maureen down there in her chair.

It happened later on in Biology. I folded up like a jackknife and fell off my stool. It was just like somebody shot me in the guts — not with a bullet exactly — more like with some kind of arrow.

They couldn't get the cyst out clean, so they kept me hooked up to the drip for a week, until everything stunk like antibiotics — my skin and my breath and my shit. The cut was held shut with black stitches and some kind of tape. I kept pushing the blanket down to see, and one time, after the nurse told me not to, I touched it. It didn't hurt. I ran my finger along it, kind of stroking, until something inside lifted up and shoved my hand away.

The Demerol turned everything slow and dark. My dad came to visit a couple of times, but he was mostly a shadow by the side of the bed, a red and black workshirt with a sawdusty cigarette smell. Maureen never showed, but I figured he didn't tell her, the way things were going the last time I saw them together. I was out in the truck, waiting for him to drive me to school. When he finally came out she was hot on his tail — she grabbed hold of the porch rail with both hands and screamed after the back of his head, 'You know it John, you're the weakest sonofabitch that's ever been!'

The day they let me go home, my dad was an hour late picking me up. I sat there in the lobby, ten pounds skinnier than the day they brought me in, feeling like a good gust of wind could pin me to the wall. For the first time ever I thought about dying. I could see it clear as anything — that even if I was only fourteen, there'd come a day when I'd up and croak.

When he finally showed up he reeked of beer. In the truck he told me how he'd found us a new house and moved our stuff in. Then out of the blue he started saying how Roberta couldn't wait to meet me. 'You remember, I told you about Roberta in the hospital. You remember.'

She was there when we got there. The first thing she did was reach into the fridge and pull out two beers and hand one to my dad. It didn't take a genius to see it was her house he'd found.

There were cases of empties towered up in the kitchen and all down the back stairs to the yard. It would've been simple as anything for me to steal a few beers, or even a case, but I didn't feel much like drinking somehow. All I wanted was sleep, but the two of them got pissed and noisy every night, waking me up so I could hear them in the shower together, her squealing, 'You dirty bastard, I'll fix your wagon!' and him laughing loud and crazy in a way I'd never heard. Thinking the water was drowning it all out I guess.

One night I woke up with my heart going crazy. Roberta was right outside my door — I could hear her out there, taking slow raspy drags and letting the smoke out in these long kind of sighs. 'Hey,' she said after a minute or so, 'we gotta keep it down.' She was just like some drunk in a movie, trying to whisper but not getting it right. 'Gotta keep it down, the kid needs her sleep.'

She could've been talking to my dad, I guess, but nobody answered her back. I lay awake after that. I shut my eyes, but all I could see was her standing out there, her yellow permed hair and her big sagging butt and her loud, lonely voice in the dark.

My dad drove me to school like always, only now we passed the new mall they were building. Seventeen new stores and a tall pointy tower with a hole for a clock to go in. Every morning I looked up at that tower with the skeleton scaffold. I saw how those men walked around up there, so free and easy, the same way my dad had to when he was building houses, when they knew the ground was down there — one false move and they were meat.

I thought about Maureen. Her straight black hair with the grey wing lifting out of the part. I thought about when I was little and still going with her to church, bowing my head for the Our Father and getting the screaming jeebies every time.

I thought about her all alone in the house at the end of the road — the house I'd lived in since I was five, when my real mom took off and Maureen, who was my mom's best friend back then, took me and my dad in to stay.

I thought about calling, but I felt like my dad would know somehow, even if I called from a friend's place, or even from the payphone in the lobby at school. Worse than that, I thought about Maureen's face. The way it cracked open when they told me, and I saw how a person's heart really was fragile, as fragile as the teacups Maureen kept on the highest shelf. From her mother's family in Ireland, she said. 'You can see clean through them in the sunlight Robin. They'll break if you don't hold them right.'

Roberta took me into their room one time when my dad was out. The bedcovers were all twisted up like somebody'd been fighting there, and there were ashtrays spilling their guts on the carpet. The curtains were pulled half open to where they stuck I guess. When Roberta put her arm around me I could smell whatever she was drinking the night before, and something hot and sour, and baby powder, and about half a can of Instant Beauty hairspray.

'I've got some sweaters and stuff I bet you'd like here Robin. What about this one?' The bulb was burnt out in the closet. She reached into the dark and pulled clothes out of the lump on the floor, until my arms were piled up to my nose and her smell was all through me, making me sick.

I had to pass by their bedroom on the way to the bathroom. I'd wake up having to go and hold it until my guts were cramping, but sooner or later I'd have to give in. It was one of those hollow veneer doors, and half the time it wasn't closed all the way. I'd hear Roberta giggling in there, or else the sound of a bottle getting knocked on the floor, or once I heard her saying, 'Fuck me, fuck me,' down deep in her throat like a dog — and then a whimper that must've been him.

After the operation, right after, I came crawling out from under the anesthetic feeling like they'd taken the wind out of me somehow, like maybe they'd cut my lungs out too. Then I started coughing, hacking up all the crap I had in my chest, and when I saw how much there was I figured I better quit smoking. The kids I knew all started up around eight or nine, in the black maples out back of the school. I knew enough to keep it hidden, until Maureen found a pack under my bed when I was twelve. 'Just don't go bumming off of me,' she told me, 'and don't even think about stealing because I'll know.' I could lift a few off my dad though, and sometimes he even gave me one and put a finger to his lips to make it our secret. Everybody I knew smoked, except really little kids. Nobody believed me when I said I was quitting. The thing was, it scared the shit out of me, coming out of that anesthetic.

I went without a smoke for a few weeks, but then one night I looked up from the TV and saw Roberta take a long drag and wash it down with a swig of beer. I saw my dad's head beside her, passed out on the back of the couch, and that's when I went in to the kitchen and took a pack out of the carton on the table. I tore my room apart looking for my lighter and when I finally found a book of matches there was only one left. When the first smoke burnt down to the filter I lit another one off the butt. I kept it up for an hour or so I guess, hacking my guts out and not really giving a shit.

One morning there was nobody out working on the new mall. We pulled up at the stoplight and I watched the wind rattle the scaffold and blow garbage under the locked-up trucks.

There was no homeroom that day — we all had to go down to the gym for assembly instead. They wouldn't say why until we were all packed in there, and then they told us to lower our heads and take a minute of silence for Darcie Lenichek. They passed a couple of photos around the bleachers for anyone who didn't know who she was. She was in my grade eight gym until she broke her thumb trying to do a cartwheel. It was creepy — the thumb was hanging off her hand but she never made a sound. Just bit her lips shut while the blood all drained out of her face.

They told us how she'd hung herself from the top of the new clock tower. And how some trucker saw her dangling up there and radioed the cops. And how the cops came and cut her down, just when the sky was getting light.

'Holy shit,' Roberta said when it came on the newsbreak that night. 'You know her Robin?'

'Not really.' I looked over at my dad's face to see what it meant to him, the picture of that girl on the screen and her having killed herself not two miles from where we sat. His eyes were closed, but I could tell by the pucker in his forehead he wasn't sleeping. He was keeping them shut on purpose.

A bunch of us went down to the cemetery on Friday night to see where Darcie was buried. It was a small headstone, almost like the ones they have for babies, and somebody said they make them like that for suicides. There was one of those styrofoam wreaths laid over the dirt, the kind they have down at the horsetrack, with ribbons and plastic flowers. We held our lighters over the grave to get a better look.

The idea was we'd walk out the old traintracks from there and light a fire, but it never ended up happening. Somebody sat down beside the grave, and then somebody else, until we made a kind of circle around it. We passed a couple of twenty-sixers around, taking long swallows and closing our throats to keep it down.

It broke up sometime after midnight. Some crawled off to fuck or get sick in the bushes, and the rest of us laughed our way out of there, past all those crosses and slabs of stone.

I ended up on my own somehow, sneaking up on every parked car and truck I came across, twisting off gascaps and hucking them into the bushes. My head filled up with fumes, filled up like a balloon and floated, tied to my neck with a string. For a second I thought about matches, or the lighter in my coat pocket, stuffed in with the smokes I had left.

That's when I saw it. Across the road, way up in the rocks at the back of the old folk's home was a tall, tall sign — all bright and hazy white. I couldn't make out the letters, but I knew well enough they wouldn't spell *Welcome.*

I was pissed. I ripped my jeans going over the fence and wiped out a few times on the rocks, bad enough to skin both palms and one knee. When I got up close and saw how the signboard was stuck to the post — two fat bolts I'd never force apart — I knew I'd have to take the whole thing. I was small for fourteen. The sign stood a good foot over my head and they'd wedged it in deep, but my mind was made up. I put my shoulder to it. Rammed up against it and fell flat on my ass and got up and rammed it again

It was about all I could carry. I had to hook it over my shoulder and drag it behind me down the road, not really knowing where I was going — or knowing, but not seeing the mistake. I was headed for the house at the end of the road. The house with the living room light on, where Maureen would be doing a crossword, not watching the TV but keeping it on.

The streetlights were planted far apart, one dying down at the corner behind me and one far ahead, laying the light down like a blanket beside the dark driveway to home. The sign was cutting into my shoulder. I wanted to lay it down easy and rest, but my fingers weren't working right — it slipped, and the racket it made ran all up and down the road. It gave me the creeps, lying there. All white and still, with dark smears of blood where my grated-up hands had touched the paint, and those letters like shiny black scars. I'll hide it under the hedge, I thought, the high black hedge that runs around the house, and the thought made me smile like a moron. I hoisted the sign up and hooked it over my shoulder again, but that was when the dark filled up with headlights, and the sound of a truck braking, and my dad's boots hitting the road.

I woke up in my old room with a bucket beside me, and a glass of water and two Tylenol pills. I cried for a minute or so when I saw that. It made me think of Maureen putting them there, and my dad behind her in the doorway, or maybe even beside her, watching her pull the covers up around my neck.

'Robin.' My dad's voice outside the door. 'Robin, get up. I need a hand.'

Roberta talked at me the whole time I was throwing our stuff into boxes. Her voice came out all sloppy — she'd been up all night, she kept saying, thinking the two of us were bleeding to death in some ditch somewhere and now this, now after all that she finds out we were at that bitch's place. 'She's turned your father's head Robin. You know he loves me. He'll be back inside of a week.'

My dad was outside in the truck. I could hear the engine running.

STITCHES

–x–x–x–x–x–x–x–

SEVEN BLACK KNOTS in the muscle at the base of my thumb.

I was asking for it I guess, cutting a kaiser that way. Never cut towards your body. Never run with the scissors, never lick a cold doorknob, and never, ever horse around beside a well. I don't know where my mind was. It must've slid sideways into some thought or other — only for a second — but a second was all it took. The knife was sharper than I thought. My hand caved open at the touch of it, the way watermelons do when they're ready.

They said down at the clinic to come back in a couple of weeks and get them out, but it's been ten days or so now, and I don't know, the cut looks well enough healed to me. I can't seem to leave them alone. I keep stretching my thumb back to pull the threads tight, and worrying the knots with my finger.

–x–

My dad cut himself in the same place once. Me and my brother were little when it happened, maybe four and three, but I remember it all the same. He was working maintenance for the railroad. White-washing barriers and replacing splintered ties and cutting the wild grass back where it tried to choke the tracks.

That's what he was doing when it happened, cutting the wild grass. The foreman called out to him from the far end of the field — or else a horsefly settled on the back of his neck, or the train whistled warning, or maybe a swallow dipped down close by and tilted its belly his way. He can never remember quite what, but some small thing happened to make him lose track.

In my head, your undershirt's pulled up like a hood, the way you wore it on hot days. Your back bends over the track, burnt and peeled and burnt again, so you're the same red-brown and shape of a deer stooping down to drink. There's a shock of grass, a yellow shock grown thick and seedy between the ties. You grab it. Your hand swings up and back behind — but this is the part I can't figure. I know it was a scythe. I know you tried to hack that grass and somehow hacked your hand instead, but when I think of it, that's not what I see. What I see is a hawk. It sits up on your cutting hand the way hunters used to train them. Eyeing your brown fist in the grass.

–x–x–

There was something wrong with that hand, the one that held the scythe. It wasn't anything you'd pick up on, unless he happened to be handling something delicate — something like a woman's scarf. Or say you caught him turning the fine pages of the almanac, or trying to force thread through a needle's eye — then you'd see. It was like the fingers weren't his. Like he'd lost his real hand to some animal, swapped it for a sorry paw.

'It's a wonder he's got the use of it,' my mother told me when I asked. 'It swelled up like a cabbage when he broke it. You think I'm joking? It was big as one, and purple too.'

(This is her memory, not mine. I was newly walking when it happened, but I've heard the story so many times I can run it through my head from start to finish, like one of those flickery films they made us watch in school.)

He was landlocked. He came inland from the coast, found work, fell head over heels and woke up a family man. One dry, mosquitoey night, he dug a pit in our sandbox and filled it with smouldering coals. He wrapped corn and fresh trout and potatoes in tinfoil and buried them deep in the sand. 'Now that's a barbecue,' he told her, 'that's how we do it back home.' Later on he dug up the silver shapes and broke open the foil. His face disappeared in the steam. 'Look at that willya, the Devil's been after our dinner.'

You were happy that night. She washed up the dishes with you pressing behind her, laying kisses on her muscular neck. You didn't hear the screen door. It was no wonder, with the radio on loud and her low voice singing and the tap running hard in the sink. I was clear across the yard by the time you looked up. Stepping barefoot into the red hot sand.

You felt the scream all through you. Your blood came up like murder — only there was nobody to kill, nobody to blame but yourself. She broke for the door, took the steps in one and sprinted, thinking you were seconds behind. But you weren't. You were still in the kitchen, hanging your head while you drove your blunt fist through the wall.

'So there were two to be taken to hospital,' is how the story always ends, and that look on her face, three parts pissed off to one part wonder, or maybe even pride. 'The crazy bugger.'

(In school, the screen rolled down out of a metal case. There was a painting on the wall there, *The Plains of Abraham*, it said, black horses, blood and fire. Whenever we watched a film I could feel it, sometimes I could even see it there, sharper than whatever was up on the screen. Nobody told me this part, but it's like that painting, hanging behind and burning through. My mother's dead center. She's carrying me with my feet tied up in bags of ice and my fists all tangled in her hair. Her face twists away to the neighbour, she's yelling, 'Watch the baby til I'm back.' In the corner of the frame, my dad comes loping. His bad hand dangles down.)

–x–x–x–

'There's nightsnakes,' Jim told us, 'and toads. You might catch warts or get bit on the heel.'

We were forbidden to go barefoot anywhere wild — anywhere like the woods and ditchy fields around the Boyle's place — but we were seven and eight. When supper was done and the parents sat back to smoke, we left our runners in the milkweed and followed Jim Boyle into the gloom.

At the black dip of the slough, Jim flicked open his jackknife, cut three cattails and set their furry heads on fire. He kept the tall one for himself and led the way, under the high poplars and out the far side to the burn. Dark was falling. Stumps stuck up black — not flat the way men make, but sharp, sheared off by the fire like giant thorns. And all around us the rustle and soft stink of fireweed. The flowers came up to our chests. Light from our torches spilt and bled on their stalky heads, staining wherever we waded bright purple in the dark.

The nail came out of nowhere. Drove in through the bottom and out through the top of my foot. I screamed and opened my mouth to scream again, but there was no air, not in my chest or anywhere else. I thrashed at the fireweed and held my torch closer to see. A half-burnt board lying low in the weeds. My foot was white, like one of those fish they find in the caves with no light, the blue veins jumping, rust and blood, the skin all bunched and puckered around the nail. Jim took one look and belted away to the house. My brother sucked his lip, backed up and sank down in the fireweed, whimpering.

Then there was quiet. Quiet like I never knew before or since, for a long time there was nothing but quiet. And that four inch nail in my foot.

My mother was the first thing I heard. Her face dangled in front of me, but her voice was far off, tangled up in something and shrieking.

Then the blue chest of his shirt. My dad stepped down on both ends of the board. His hands came up under my arms. 'Brave girl,' he said, 'that's a brave girl.' And fast, like you rip off a bandaid, he lifted me free.

–x–x–x–x–

Three years later, my mother was making her mind up to leave. She was lying awake nights, untying the knots that held her to the family the four of us made, to the coast house they'd saved for, to him. We all knew it. It spread out through the house like a smell — like something terrible left on the stove, a pot full of animal parts and black mushrooms, and that spidery hair that grows on trees.

My dad took us down to the beach all the time. We dug buckets of clams and shucked them and brought her the yellow guts, but she left them on the counter. Stood staring out the window while the cat jumped up and crouched and wolfed them down.

He taught us to cast. My brother caught on in a few tries — he could flick the rod and send the lure flying, with hardly a splash where it hit the sea. But nothing bit. He got sick of waiting, handed the rod back to my dad and walked off to squat down by the tidepools, stick his finger in the anemones and rip limpets away from their rocks.

I couldn't get the hang of it. My dad told me over and over, stood behind me and moved my hands and arms to show me how, which only made it worse. The lure wouldn't fly more than ten feet. It jerked on the end of the line, kicked up like it was dying, ripped open the surface and sank like a stone. He moved a ways down the beach. He kept on saying what he'd already said, but his voice slowed down and his eyes were nowhere near what I was doing. It made me desperate. I hauled the rod over my shoulder and cracked it like a whip, the line hissed and the lure shot through the sky, a perfect arc — until it banked. It did. Just like the sky was the sea and that lure was a living fish, it banked and swam straight back at his eyes.

His arm came up fast. He stumbled back a few steps, just a few, but the pebbles were wet and kelpy, and he lost his feet and fell. The lure sailed over him, sunk its hooks into a log and hung there like a silvery leech. He was all twisted up. 'Get your mother,' he said low, and he pulled a funny face that made me laugh. 'Get your mother!' he screamed, 'I've broken my leg!'

(My rubber boots were a size too big, I remember, they fell away from my feet as I ran.)

It was broken in two places. Greenstick in the thigh and the shin cracked through. The ligaments and tendons all torn. She couldn't leave him like that, dragging his cast like a run-over dog. She had to be patient.

−X−X−X−X−X−

The year my dad married his new wife, he walked off a buddy's porch and fell twelve feet in the dark. No time to think about bending his knees. It was poker night. Somebody was in the can for the long haul, so my dad went outside to find a bush. Nobody mentioned the renovations. It was a beautiful night. He looked up at the stars and stepped off where the back stairs had been.

He compressed a couple of bones in his spine. In my head they were small, like the backbone segments in the salmon my mother used to can, turned soft with a drop of vinegar to save picking them out.

He was in bed for more than a month, going crazy with painkillers and pain. On Fridays my mother dropped us off at the foot of their gravel drive. We passed those weekends like a couple of retrievers, brought in for sleep and feedings, and made to sit quiet while he mumbled and stroked our heads.

He recovered. He could walk and work and laugh and drink and even go line dancing again. You'd never guess it happened. Except for his height. He was shorter by an inch and a bit.

(I was sixteen the night I walked off a cliff. It was a beach party.

I don't remember it myself — I was too loaded — but my boyfriend told me all there was to know. 'You walked offa there like you thought you could fly,' he kept saying, and after a while it got funny. We were lying on the sand in the first morning light, with his hand in my jeans and my ankle puffed up, turning purple from the inside out.)

–x–x–x–x–x–x–x–

Something happened to you when you were laid up those long weeks with your back. It was late afternoon, with your wife out for groceries and the place to yourself. Death came to the window. That's what you told me — Death came right to the window, reached in through the curtains and grabbed hold of your foot. 'The hand wasn't icy,' you said. 'It wasn't long and bony either, like you might think. It was warm. A little hot even, and hard, the way my hands got when I worked on the rails. You remember?'

You fought it. You fought like hell, kicking and swinging out with your fists, until finger by finger, you won.

–x–x–x–x–x–x–x–

Me and my brother were little when it happened.

We were alone with my dad. My mother must've been getting the dessert — there were cupboards opening on the far side of the kitchen door, and the sound of something good getting spooned into four small bowls.

My dad laid down his fork. He held his fist out to us finger-side down, the way that meant candy or some other surprise. He stroked his wild beard and smiled, but when he opened his hand there was nothing. Nothing but the ragged black stitches we'd already seen — we'd made him show us ten times a day since he came home from the company clinic with blood on the heel of his hand.

He took hold of his steak knife, slid the tip under the stitches and cut the first loop. After that it was simple. He cut and pried, took a breath and cut and pried again, then pinched one end and peeled them from the flesh of his hand.

He held them up to the light. Then laid them on the table in front of us.

My mother was pissed off when she saw what he'd done. 'For Christ's sake Daniel,' she grabbed them up in her dishtowel, 'you'll scare them.'

But we knew what he meant.

C L U E S

1. TONYA PODOLSKY had yellow hair — the kind I wanted — thick as sheaves of wheat, with bangs flipping back from her wide blue eyes. Breasts too. Bigger than any girl in our grade, and Mama said that's why she stood that way, with her shoulders curled forward like she was cold.

No use having them if you don't stand straight, Mama told me. *You show what God gave you, it's a gift.* I looked down over my lowly beginnings, a couple of fried eggs in my shirt. *Oh you'll get 'em,* she said, *women in my line have always had shape.* She cupped a hand under one of her own then, lifted it and let it fall.

The boys didn't notice Tonya's shoulders — they were too busy watching her chest, or her behind in those raggedy cut-offs she wore. My long sweet legs were nothing, not when Tonya looked up at them through her flower-blue eyes. She spoke some kind of language — one I couldn't even hear — like those high-up whistles that make a dog swivel its ears.

2. You couldn't see where she got it. Her whole family was ugly, the mother flat-chested with a twig-line mouth, slacks flapping like laundry on her legs. She took forever to do anything — hanging her head over the dishes, dragging weeds from the dirt, droning over the

back fence to the lady next door. *Her best friend,* Tonya said, *like you and me.*

The neighbour lady talked high and sweet. *Isn't that the way,* she'd say, or *wouldn't you know it,* or sometimes even *I declare.* She was fat, with friendly hands and clown-red hair wound up on the top of her head. Her man came and went in the night, but we could tell when he was home, his purple rig squashing the couchgrass, dwarfing the rest of the road.

3. Outside of the vegetable patch, the yard was dust, torn up by the dogs and the chickens and Tonya's two brothers on their BMX bikes. They played with danger, tailpipes and bottles, jaggedy open-mouth cans. They watched me — time and again I caught the two of them watching, that yellow hair flat to their heads.

Tonya watched Mama. *You're so lucky,* she told me, even though other kids felt sorry for me, having no dad. Whenever she came to the apartment, Tonya watched Mama like a hawk. Like a poor kid watches your sandwich in school, no matter if it's only baloney or jam.

4. The father was never inside. He was with his animals out back, or out front with his bust-open rowboat, his motorbike bones and the rusted-out corpses of cars. Bent like a man twice his age — grease in his wrinkles and black like a burn on his hands. His beard ran down to a rat-tail point, and when he stooped over an engine or an animal, he tied it up short in a knot.

He'd built on to the back shed. The chicken coop stuck out from its side, plywood and milk crates, car doors and chicken wire and tires. The hens were dirty mop heads, turning up trash in the yard. One cut its foot on an old fuse, and we watched as he crept up to it, so slow and gentle it stood blinking in the dust. It didn't peck at the bandage — just sat healing in the straw, even laid him a fine brown egg. We watched him reach in under its feathers. It never even let out a sound.

5. Once, the little brother grabbed my behind. When I whirled on him he just stood there, blue eyes slitty, slipping side to side in his face. The mother saw, but she turned back to her runner beans like she couldn't care less. Then later, he came running and jumping, and she met him with the back of her hand.

6. The back shed smelled like zoo. The father kept cockatoos and canaries, and lizards under heat lamps — a yard-long iguana, a chameleon with wandering eyes. The lovebirds had the biggest cage. He laid his cheek to the wire, talking foreign to them, sometimes even singing. They came close, edged one after the other down their long dead branch and leaned out to his music, touching their red beaks to his lips. He forgot we were there. He must've. When he finally stood back, the cage left a pattern on his face.

7. Tonya had a tiny room. No dresser, no bed even, just a mattress on the floor. Everything she had was in boxes, lined up down the gyprock wall. There was a secret at the bottom of her sock box — a tube of lipstick, taken from the neighbour lady's purse. It twisted out shapely and perfect, a pole of Pagoda Red.

We were being Blondie, me on air guitar and Tonya up front, rewinding her beat-up deck. She had the lipstick on and a loose black tank top with no bra. Her red lips mouthing, *Once had a love it was a gas. Soon turned out, had a heart of glass.*

There was no lock on the door, no handle even, just a hole where the handle should've been. Tonya'd stuffed a sock in there and taped over it, so the boys wouldn't watch her, down on their knees in the hall. The boxes we'd wedged up to the door slid forward and spun. Tonya dove for the stop button, smearing her mouth with the heel of her hand. Her mother came on slow, dirty fingers rising up to hook in under Tonya's jaw. *Where'd you get it?*

Tonya blinked like her mother was a bright light.

You answer me Tonya.

I — Paula. It's Paula's.

I froze. I was a bad liar — I'd given up trying with Mama. Tonya's mother turned to me and I nodded, feeling out behind me for the wall.

She pressed her lips to Tonya's ear. *If you're lying*, she said low. Then she let go. Tonya stumbled on the lip of the mattress. She fell back into the blankets and her tank top flipped up, flashing one of her nipples, lonely and fingertip pink.

Get it off. Her mother paused at the door. *You look like a five dollar fuck.*

8. Sleeping over, I had to share Tonya's mattress. She laced her fingers through mine under the blankets and wouldn't let go. We listened to her brothers through the makeshift wall, making animal sounds in their sheets, calling each other *cocksucker* and *shitlick*, until the mother yelled out for them to shut up.

I woke up with my hand empty. Tonya was at the window, moonlight coming white through her nightie, making the top of her head glow cold.

Tonya?

She touched the tip of her finger to the screen.

You could see clean through the scraggy trees, the slanted fence and the flapping sheers. The neighbour lady down on her knees. Her high hair flat under the truck man's hands, him humping her face like a dog.

9. The road they lived on wasn't paved yet. It was gravel at first, but it gave way to dirt where it curled into the country at the edge of town. The Braemar boys called out as we passed. They were older, the youngest of them at least fifteen.

Hey Tonya. Ton - ya. C'mere for a sec. C'mere.

The three of them planted in a row, arms folded on their farmboy chests. Tonya took the ditch like a deer and stood facing them, while I rustled in the milkweed behind.

You wanna see our treehouse?

We built it ourselves.

I didn't answer. They weren't asking me, and anyway, my voice had dried out. I'd have to spit to speak, the words blood-brown and crumbly, like the worms in the dust at my feet.

When Tonya spoke it was so sweet, so low the three of them had to lean forward, close in on her to hear what she said. *Sure*, she said, *sure. I'd love it.*

She was first on the ladder, the oldest pushing the others aside, his head tilting to see into the shadows of her shorts. *How old're you anyways?* he called up to her behind.

Fourteen, she sang, easing up through the hole in the treehouse floor.

Liar, I tried to call after her. But all that came out of me was a croak.

10. There were gerbils in the shed, a mass of them tangled in their cage.

You think pets? The father said, kneeling down beside me. *Is no pets. Give snake dead gerbil he no think food. No fresh enough for snake.*

He kept it in a glass tank. Bigger than any fish tank, but the snake was enormous — it had to fold back on itself in a patterned pile. A boa constrictor. I saw myself in the jungle, saw it dropping on me, winding, like being hugged to death, no air. Then the sound of my ribs snapping. Driving their white ends through my heart.

You feed? he asked me, and behind him, Tonya grinned. She was always behind him, a little to one side, like a soldier. He sprung the latch on the top of the gerbil cage, reached in and grabbed one, closing his black hand tight.

C'mon, said Tonya, *it's easy.*

Its head stuck out from his fist. The black eyes met mine and I shook my head silently, no.

He motioned for Tonya to draw back the lid. His arm swung out like a crane, fingers squeezing the gerbil to make it squeak. The snake's eye snapped open. He spread his hand and the gerbil sprang, rebounding off a scaly coil. Tonya slid the lid back. The seconds stretched out, the boa lowering its eyes to half-mast, the gerbil frantic, running laps with its shoulder to the glass. It happened like the crack of a whip. There was no squeezing — no need with a meal so small — just open and swallow it whole.

We watched it go down, a lump in the snake's long throat, struggling for a second, then still.

11. The whirlpool was like cooking in a cannibal pot. It made my head hang sick, but Tonya kept at me until I gave in. There were boys in the big pool. I'd be left with them, in my bathing suit, alone.

Tonya's breasts rode high in her bikini, blown up under the water's bubbling skin. *Sit over a jet,* she mouthed at me, grinning.

A woman hauled herself out — wobbling thighs, clumsy, like a seal on land. We were alone with a man. He was old, somewhere between father and grandfather, his shoulder hair curling up grey. He looked from Tonya to me, then back, the way men did, to her. *You girls like the whirlpool?* he asked. *Like the whirl?*

Tonya smiled at him sideways, silent under her trickling hair.

The water was foaming, and maybe he thought I couldn't see. His arm swimming pink and grey, like a salmon when it's spawning, rotting and dropping its skin. The hooked mouth hand eased into the V in her lap, and when I looked up to meet them, Tonya's perfect blue eyes had gone blank.

He climbed out dripping, trunks dragging on his wide behind.

She was quiet in the showers. Soaping herself all over, rinsing and soaping again.

12. Mama was cleaning the apartment. She told us to get some fresh air, but there was a fort in the basement, a cave under the foot of the stairs. The carpet was darker there, never walked on before. We traced the pattern with our fingers, black winding through patches of gold.

We could live here, Tonya whispered, and then she hugged me, so hard I could barely breathe. I struggled, not much, but she pushed me away, stood suddenly and split her scalp on the sharp under-edge of a stair. Blood spread out from her crown, drowning her dense yellow hair.

Mama held Tonya the whole way there, a fresh towel clamped hard, the first one lying red on our floor. Tonya wouldn't look at me. She cried like she was dying, her face buried in Mama's green dress.

At the hospital she screamed and scrambled back when the doctor came close, reaching out with his wide-knuckled hand. She held fast to Mama's arm, so Mama dug for a quarter, and told me what to say.

I let it ring and ring. I could see them — her kneeling in the dirt, the boys wheeling, him bent in his filthy shed. Not one of them answering. Not one of them looking up at the sound.

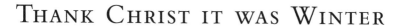

THANK CHRIST IT WAS WINTER

I'VE GOT NOTHING against Indians. At least I didn't, until a family of them moved into the other half of the duplex me and my wife Sherry were renting.

The day they showed up, I stood and watched from the living room window. He was stumbling around the way they do, yelling at her and the kids, yelling things I couldn't understand. She just kept her eyes to the ground and unloaded the car. The kids must've been cold without coats — it was the tail end of September, and winter doesn't wait much longer than that in Whitehorse. But then I've heard Indians can take the cold better. It's in their genes.

Long after they'd all gone inside, I stood there watching, like my feet were stuck to the floor, until Sherry tugged at the back of my shirt and pulled me round for a kiss. Great, I said. I know, said Sherry, don't let it get to you. She's like that, Sherry — she was seven months into her term then, and still serving at the Taku. The guys down there were starting to give her a hard time about her belly, but she didn't let it get to her. Those buttheads don't know an ass from an elbow, she'd tell me, and grin.

A day or two after they moved in was the first time I heard him beat her up. The walls were cardboard in that place, and I could hear their voices, his like a grizzly and hers like a chainsaw whining into a knot. The voices went back and forth, sometimes with long gaps between, where they were ignoring each other, or maybe just forgetting where they were. And then he hit her, and it made a sound that couldn't be anything else. I put the paper down, stood up and went to the wall. The blood was coming hard and fast in my ears, I remember, and I felt weak. Then he hit her again, again, and then she fell to the floor and cried out, and I remembered the time I hit a doe in my truck, late at night, coming round the last bend before town. I thought I heard one of the kids start to cry. I put my hands to the wall. I stood there with my hands pressed flat on the wall and I waited. Then I heard the front door slam, and him staggering down the steps, and then it was like I could see through the wall, like I could see her lying there in a ball, with her black hair fallen over the swelling side of her face. But of course I couldn't.

When Sherry got home from shopping I was back in the armchair. I told her about it and she shook her head, then pulled open the cupboard and started putting stuff away.

The next time it happened was maybe a week and a half later, and Sherry was home with me, doing her cross-stitch while we watched TV. She was leaned back into the sofa with her belly sticking out, and when she caught me looking sideways at it she said, I know, I'm getting big as a barn. I wanted to let her know I felt good looking at it, her belly, the baby. But I couldn't find a way to say it. And then they started up next door and the thought left my mind.

You hear? I said, and she nodded, pressing her lips tight. We both sat forward on the couch and listened, heard her hit the wall, then a bottle break, or maybe a glass. I almost stood, but Sherry's hand was on my knee, holding me. Wait, she said, I think it's stopped. And she was right, there was quiet. On my way to the kitchen to get another pack from the carton, I looked out the front door window. The kids were on their half of the porch — the boy moving a dump truck over the boards and the girl standing still, looking away to the North, the way the wind was coming from.

It happened regularly after that, almost once a week, and it always stopped just before I could decide on what to do. Sherry always shook her head, and one night, just after we'd heard the woman hit the floor, and heard him leave, and turned up the radio so we couldn't hear her crying, Sherry said, Jesus Jim, I wish to hell you'd get some work so we could get out of this dump. She went in to the bedroom then and when I crawled in later she was asleep, turned away from my side of the bed.

It wasn't long after that I got a call from Norm at Yukon Electrical. He said Dave Roberts had taken to his bed with pneumonia, and he needed somebody to fill in. There were lines down all around town and clear up the highway — last night's storm was a sonofabitch. This could be your in Jimmy, he said, I've been looking to transfer Roberts. I said great, and I knew without asking that I'd meet up with him and the others at the McDonald's the next morning, seven AM, the way I had in spring before the lay-offs. I called Sherry at the bar, and when I told her she let out a whoop and I could hear men laughing in the background. I said, I love you honey, over the phone and she was quiet for a minute because neither of us had ever done that. Then she said, Me too, and hung up.

The next morning I was surprised at how deep the snow was, and it made me realize I hadn't been out in over a week. I shovelled the walk and threw down salt, scraped the windshield, breathed deep the splintery-cold November air and felt like a new man. Backing out of the drive I saw the Indians had nailed up some sheets for curtains. They covered the front window completely, except for the bottom corner, where the little girl had her brown face pressed into the glass. I looked away, over my shoulder as I backed out into the road.

At the McDonalds everything was the same as in spring, only the guys were wearing boots and had their parkas slung over the backs of the yellow swivel chairs. Norm told me I'd be riding with him, and I knew that meant I'd be doing the grunt work, but I didn't care — I felt so good to be there with those men, breathing the warm egg and sausage smell, knowing I had work.

Norm was good company. We talked about the Hockey, the Chevy he had an eye on, the latest bullshit stunt his wife had pulled, charging up a fortune on new carpets when they'd had them done three years before. I'm telling you, Jimmy, he said, there's nothing like a woman to keep you broke. I don't know how it came around, but I ended up telling him about the Indians next door, the way he staggered around the yard, the way he hit her, the sounds they made, the kids. Norm pulled out onto the highway, rolling the wheel with the heel of his hand, reaching into the chest pocket of his vest to pull out a Players. Those bastards, he said. You think I should do something? I asked. Not a damn thing you can do, he said, even if you called the RCMP and had him taken away, or say you took her down to the shelter they've got going at the hospital. She'd be right back there the next day and she'd hate your guts for the shit she'd get. I've seen it a hundred times. When I used to drive cab I had one of them start beating his woman in the back of the car. They were both loaded and he was calling her a bitch and a slut and everything else under the sun. I finally pulled over and told him to get out. Of course he wouldn't, so I stepped out to give him a hand. I'll be damned if she didn't crawl out the other side and come up behind me with her claws out. Leave him alone she screams in my ear, and I turn and see she's got a shiner around one eye, and a cut lip, and blood running out her nose. Leave him alone, she screams, so I pushed him into the ditch and her after him and I left them there. I see them in front of the liquor store still. Still together. You see what I'm saying Jimmy?

We were covering the lines up the hill from town, along the stretch of highway that leads to McIntyre, the new reservation. It's like a suburb — they've got some houses in there I wouldn't say no to. Sherry and me were living in a mixed part of town then, under the cliffs that reach up to the airport. Whenever a plane went over you couldn't even hear the TV.

Norm pulled the truck over beside a pole with a line swinging loose in the wind. I knew I'd be the one to climb it so I did up my coat and reached for my boots. Norm grinned when I jumped out, then he picked up his clipboard to look busy.

I waded into the ditch, up to my knees, waist, even my chest at one place where the wind had pushed the snow into a drift like the crest of a wave. The pole was frozen and slippery, but I climbed it easy enough, dug my spurs in and didn't waste time — I knew Norm'd be watching. At the top I opened the fuse, identified the line, made sure it was dead. I could feel the wind moving the pole, and the thought came to me, I wonder if the wind moved the cross when Jesus hung up there. I wonder if he could feel the wind pulling at his cross, and maybe he hoped it might snap and send him slamming to the ground before anything else killed him, the thorns or the nails or the hunger.

The line was whipping in the wind now, flipping and twisting like a weasel in a trap. I reached for it, but it jumped away from my hand like it knew I was there, so I slammed each spur in hard and leaned out as far as I could. When it finally swung close, I caught it — just as it reared up in a gust and touched its tail to the live line overhead. I felt it kick like a black snake in my hand, watched the tail turn back on me like a mouth.

The shock threw me right off the pole. I was in the air for what seemed like minutes, like one of those slow motion ice-tea drinkers on the commercial, falling backwards into a pool. Whenever I tell the story, Sherry says Thank Christ it was winter, if it wasn't for all that snow the fall would've snapped his neck for sure.

Norm dug me out, picked me up and carried me to the truck, holding me gently, like you hold a sleeping child. After they checked me out at the hospital he drove me home, where we found the Indian flat on his face in the snow, on our side of the yard. Bastard, I said under my breath, and Norm laughed, but I knew as soon as my feet hit the ground he was dead. No matter how dead drunk a body is, it looks different when it's really dead. I bent down and rolled him on his side to make sure, and Norm stopped grinning when he saw how the Indian's mouth was stuffed with snow — like he'd been trying to eat it, or breathe it in.

When I called hello on their side of the porch, the little girl opened the door slowly and said, Mama sleeping, and then her dark eyes went past me to find her father in the snow. I unlocked the door to my place and stepped in to use the hallway phone, and when the operator came on the line I felt the child's arms close around my leg. I looked down on her thin black hair, then I looked out to where the dead man lay and Norm stood with his eyes turned to the sky, watching the belly of a plane pass over us all.

REDBREAST

Sure I looked up when he walked in — every girl in the place did.

Situations like that, I tend to keep still. A glass falls, I just watch it go. Inside me I'm grabbing the air where it was, dropping down on my knees and just missing and cursing and cutting my hand when it hits, but the whole time the outside just stands there.

I'd never seen a beautiful man. He was so tall he had to bend through the door — that's what I saw when I looked up, him bending through the door and springing back like a sapling birch. And his hair. Long, fall-coloured hair and branching white hands, a black helmet hanging and brown leather leggings worn thin on his thighs.

Lenore was already wiggling over to him, and that looked like the end of it. There was a saying about Lenore — it's her party and she'll fuck who she wants to. Usually in her folks' bed, smack under the sacred bleeding heart. I remember her saying how it just killed her, thinking of the two of them lying there, maybe fighting over the remote, right where she'd squealed herself stupid with dozens of creeps.

His eyes flicked over the room. Over the tall-boy beer cans and the boys, over Lenore and the candles and so many wet-mouth girls I had to look away. That's when I felt it. I felt his look land — just the same as a dragonfly lands when you're flat on your back on the dock. The stick legs tickling and the wind of its wings on your face.

He lived by the river, across the dirt road from the detox center the Uniteds had going in some rickety old school. I stood behind him while he stuck his key in the lock, with the road still swaying in my head, swinging up the corners — the two of us leaning into it like he told me, me pressing into his back and tilting, the whole time dying to lean the other way.

It was more of a shack than a house, the kind they put up so miners and their families could catch pneumonia in winter and bail out the crawlspace in spring. Leif snapped on the light. There were spiders in the beams, puffy white egg sacs and years of weaving. There was no door to his room, just a Union Jack tacked to the frame. The bathroom had one of those accordion doors, and the only other doorway was dark. It pulled at me, the way a cave mouth pulls when you're a kid. It smelled like a cave too, like something might sleep in there, only you wouldn't know until it was too late, until you touched its hairy side with your foot.

Leif leaned out for my hand. 'C'mon.' He was lifting the flag. 'Damon'll be out for a while yet.'

His bed was a green foam on the floor, with the undersheet peeling and one of those blankets that burns your skin. There was a black Led Zep flag on the wall, and a poster of some girl butt-naked except for a motorbike helmet and boots. Each one of her tits was about as big as my head, and for a second I thought about ripping her down, so he couldn't look up and compare them to mine. He spread a hand out where he wanted me, and I went and lay down. There was no way there was insulation in that place. You could feel the wind coming up through the floorboards, and the bed smelled skunky, like an old kitchen sponge.

I could tell he was wondering if it was my first time, the way he eased into me, and I knew enough to act like whatever I did was just God-given talent. I wasn't ready for what happened. The other times, the guy just grunted and fell forward like somebody'd sledgehammered the back of his head, or else pulled back on his knees and zipped it. Not Leif. Leif said my name. He'd only met me an hour before, but he said my name when he came — Robin oh Jesus Robin — and I'd never heard it said like that before, like it meant something.

He kept inside me when he was done, and I could feel him in there, turning soft and small.

What woke me was the cold on my leg. Leif was passed out with his arm flung out dead on my chest. The room was all shadowy, with light coming weak through the flag. There was a shape at the side of the bed. Not just a shadow — a shape — something hunkered down, and maybe I was dreaming or still drunk, but I could swear it was lifting the blanket. It was breathing. I could hear it, in-out, and then I could feel its breath on my thigh. I played dead — not because I decided to, but like I said, when in doubt, I tend to keep still. The blanket dropped. The shape stood up, thick and black with its arms spread wide in the red and blue web of light. I watched it in my lashes. I watched until it backed away staggering and fought its way out through the flag.

Leif. Leif was coming to pick me up. I kept cutting the thought up to make it smaller, but it was like worms — every piece grew a new head or tail, until my skull was crammed full and crawling.

I was setting myself up for a fall. He was older, sure, but he was still a guy. They talked poetry when they had your jeans down, then woke up like sleepwalkers and headed for home. Like Lenore was always saying — hard cock, soft song. Soft cock, so long.

MASH was on, and Frank was painting Hotlips' toenails red when I heard the bike. He pulled up under the window and ran the revs high to bring me out. My dad kept glued to the TV, but Maureen laid down her *Woman's Weekly* and parted the curtain to get a look.

'Jesus.' She eyeballed me over the tops of her glasses.

Outside the Rod & Gun, Leif caught hold of my arm. 'Anybody IDs you, just tell 'em you lost your purse.'

I squinted up at him — he had to be a foot taller than me at least. 'You think this is my first time in a bar?'

I wasn't dressed up or anything. I had on the same red mack and jeans as always, my hair just hanging and no makeup besides the black around my eyes — but I wasn't worried. I had an old face. People had been saying it since I was a baby. *Old soul* was what my mother called me before she left, only now I don't know if I remember that myself, or if Maureen or my dad told me, or if maybe I just made it up.

Leif was teaching me how to shoot darts when Damon showed. I knew him from across the room — the same shape in Leif's doorway, backlit like some psycho in the movies. The same shape crouching to get a look at me naked in bed.

He was still in his work clothes — cement-caked boots and paint chips in his beard and a line on his forehead where the hardhat dug in. It was dangling now, red in his hairy black knuckles. He tossed it on the table, and the three of us watched it roll around like somebody's cut-off head.

'Iceman,' he said to Leif, 'you never told me you were in love.'

Leif let out this yelp that was supposed to be a laugh. 'Love? Shit buddy, I only met her last night.'

I started drawing a circle in my palm with the tip of a dart. Damon looked me up and down, like I was some animal that wanted skinning, and he was just figuring the best place to start. 'Met her — or made her?'

Leif started with the yelping again, only this time he kept it up. I dug the tip in a little. The circle started to go pink where blood was rising up under the skin.

'This calls for a celebration.' Damon had his darts out, jamming the feathery tails in the shafts. 'Who's buyin? You buyin Ice? She's your girl right?'

Leif didn't answer. I pulled the dart away from my hand and watched a ball of blood well up where I'd broken through. Damon grabbed the shaft from my fingers.

'Leif tell you he's gettin his papers?' He flicked his bull wrist and drove the dart into the board, just inside the wire on a triple. 'Gonna be a journeyman. Yessir. Me, I'm still in demolition.'

Leif was backing away. 'It's on me buddy.' Then, like an afterthought, 'You want another one Robin?'

I nodded, but he was already gone. Damon reached past me for Leif's pack of smokes. When he pulled his hand back, the knots in his forearm brushed my front. My nipples sat up like a couple of dogs.

'Robin, huh?' He let the cigarette hang off his lip and planted his boots at the shooting line. 'Robin Redbreast.'

Leif was down the far end of the room, hung over the bar where some woman was pulling his beers.

'See that one he's talkin to? Behind the bar?' Damon was facing the other way, but God knows he was the kind to have eyes in the back of his head. She was pretty — long yellow hair and tits pushing up out of her shirt.

'That's Joelle.' Thk. Thk. Thk. He closed the sixteens. 'Her and Ice were sweethearts in high school, round about your age I guess. He was gonna marry her even. She wasn't pregnant or nothin, he just wanted it.' He was up close to the board now, plucking his darts out of the cork. 'You know what happened?'

'No.'

'Well I'll tell ya.' He turned to face me, walking slowly, his black eyes drilling holes in mine. 'He asked her — got down on his knees in this very bar, had the ring in a little pink box in his pocket.' Then he laid his arm across my shoulders, and it was harder and heavier than any flesh I'd ever felt. 'The little bitch said no. Can you believe that? No reason or nothin — just no.'

Leif was reaching in his back pocket to pay. Joelle was wiping the bar in front of him, making little figure-eights with her rag. Damon brought his mouth closer, so close I could hear it moving, rustling like a bird in his beard. 'You wouldn't do that, wouldja Redbreast? You'd marry Iceman if he asked ya?'

Leif was making his way back through the tables, two mugs sudsing over in his left hand and one in his right. Women were watching him. All through the bar, faces tilting and turning, just like they were sunflowers and Leif was the sun.

I shook Damon's arm off and stepped up to the line. 'I'm not marrying anybody.' I said it real quiet, but he heard me all the same.

'Is that a fact?' His hand came up hard under my elbow — almost a slap — lifting it so the dart in my fingers came flush with the line of my eye. 'That's it,' he said. 'Now all you gotta do is look where you want it to go.'

Leif ended up taking me home the long way, down the tunnel of black maples along the river road. About half-way there he swung off and followed a dirt track until the saplings choked in. When he cut the motor you could hear water jumping over the rocks. There was a sliver moon. The ground was wet and springy, and where we lay down you could smell horsetails and mushrooms and rotted down cottonwood leaves. Leif laid his jacket down under me but my ass got wet anyway — it was numb and marked all over with sticks before long.

After, Leif lay on his back beside me, one hand flipping a mickey to his mouth and the other one warm in my jeans. That was something. A guy keeping his hand there, still wanting to touch it when he's done. The bike was close by, watching over us like some black and chrome dog. I lifted a wet spade-shaped leaf and laid it down flat on his forehead.

'Leaf,' I said to him, 'Leif. What kinda name is that anyway?'

'Whaddaya mean? It's Viking. Erik the Red, Leif Eriksson. Shit, I never got my grade twelve and even I know that.'

I swivelled the leaf around, so it was like a heart with a stem, the pointy end dipping down between his eyes. 'What about Iceman?' I didn't think it. My mouth just opened and the words walked out.

'Huh?'

'Damon. He called you Iceman. Ice.'

'Yah.' He passed me the bottle. 'That's from when we were working up north on the pipelines.' His hand backed up out of my pants. 'There was one time I stayed working on the same spot for so long I froze to the pipe. Like this.' He curved his arms and legs out wide in the air, like a monkey holding on to its fat mother. 'Damon found me like that. He had to fire up his kerosene burner and melt snow and heat it, you know, like you get a kid's tongue off a doorknob. No shit. He melted me offa that pipe.' His voice made a weird dip, but it was too dark to see anything more than the outline of his face. 'He carried me to the truck and drove me back to camp. Took a while in front of the stove before I could move.'

A cloud went over the moon, and suddenly you couldn't tell if your eyes were open or shut. I could see it — the two of them white from head to toe, Damon breaking Leif's body away from the pipe, Leif keeping its shape, cramped in the cab, then melting, going soft by the hot black stove.

The week before I'd never laid eyes on Leif. Now I was carrying the idea of him around school with me like a doll. It made the hallways seem shorter somehow.

Lenore was in my biology, and usually she'd get us both in shit by not shutting up, but now she wouldn't even turn round. The back of her hair was teased out like something blowing up.

The teacher's legs were all eaten away, so all she had left were two sticks, kind of spotty, stuck up underneath her skirt. She had these metal canes on handcuffs, and she was dragging herself back and forth in front of the board, going on in her choirboy voice. It was something about the heart, compartments or something, but I couldn't seem to follow. I kept sliding down in my chair.

If only —

I'd hear the bike from a long way off, like the hum in a traintrack when you lay your ear flat to the rail. He'd peel up the black lick of road and pull up where the sign says NO STOPPING. His bootheels like gunshots, like thunder in the hall — he'd know where to find me, he'd kick down the door and —

Oh Jesus. That shape. Spread out like a spider in the doorway of my brain.

The wolf-whistle dropped down out of the sky. There were other girls at the bus stop, girls in tight jeans and heels — one with a rabbit fur jacket — but somehow I knew it was mine.

I looked up. The old Scotiabank was half rubble. Damon was high up on the ledge of a smashed-out window, with the walls winding down like staircases all round. He was covered in stone dust — white on his work pants, his forearms, the folds of his rolled-up sleeves. His steel-toed boots were splayed. His beard had turned grey and his hardhat stuck up like a skull.

His hand came up to wave. Mine lifted like a mirror, then stopped dead, as his swung down to cup his crotch.

I froze. I just stood there, holding my hand up in some kind of salute while he gave it a good long feel. The bus pulled up. When my arm finally dropped down, it didn't feel right. It kind of swivelled — like a Barbie arm — all hard and pink and dead.

Leif didn't answer my knock. I was trying to get a look past the shower curtain they had up over the window, when I heard him calling out, 'It's open.'

He was nowhere when I swung open the door, so I stuck my

head in through the flag. He was laying on top of the blanket, with one hand wrapped around a beer and the other one propped up on a pillow, bandaged to twice its size.

'Shit, Leif.' There was no chair, so I threw my mack over a milk crate and sat on that. 'What happened to your hand?'

'This?' He lifted it up at me and waved it. The light through his window was watery and green. 'Shark bite.'

'Come on.' I looked around. 'Where's Damon?'

He turned his face away. That's when I saw it. Piled up in the corner like some little shrine — a gold-painted picture frame twisted and burnt. Ashes and pieces of glass.

'What's that?'

'You wanna beer?' He let his empty tilt and fall off his chest, then reached into the case by my feet. I took the warm bottle from his hand. I could feel the grid of the milk crate pressing a pattern into my ass. 'What happened Leif?'

It was like he couldn't hear me. 'I forgot to tell you,' he said, 'there's this thing at the union hall on Saturday.'

The beer was rank going down. 'Yah?'

'Yah. I'll pick you up.' The hand was back on its pillow now, whiter than the pillow case, curled like it was trying to sleep. 'Wear a dress or somethin willya. Wear somethin nice.'

I was in the library at school. That was weird enough, but what I was doing there was even weirder. I had out the old school annuals, *The Centralion* they called it, for Central high. I got seven years back before I found them. Just like Damon said — high school sweethearts on the bleachers out back of the school. Not a club or a team or anything, just a bunch of bad students hanging out. Leif was thinner, with hair so shaggy you could barely make out his face. Joelle holding his white hand in the lap of her jeans. Damon behind them, one row up in a shadow. Without the beard his mouth looked full and red. His eyelids were pulled down like hoods. I looked closer.

He was hiding his thick fingers in Joelle's feathered hair.

It was near last call. I'd had more than enough, but Leif was loaded, hunkered down in his chair with his bandaged hand bumping my crotch. He was staring over my head at the bar.

I twisted round. Damon was planted on a barstool smack in front of Joelle. She was tilting her shiny mouth back and laughing, then ducking her head to sneak a shot behind the bar. She filled his shot too, her wrist easy, the way it goes when nobody's keeping track. There was hardly anyone left in the place, and it got to feeling like they were the center — some great movie on TV — and the rest of us corpses in our chairs. Joelle laughed again, only this time she spit and dribbled a shot down her front. Damon grabbed her bar rag and started wiping, polishing the tanned top-halves of her tits.

I snuck a look at Leif's face, but it wasn't there. He was on his feet, winding through the tables, his one good hand held out like he was feeling the way. At first I kept still, but then it was like something slid under my butt and lifted me, and I was behind him, close enough to hear his breath coming hard.

'Slut!' He meant it to sound mean I guess, but it caught on something in his throat and came out in two halves. Joelle's mouth made an empty little o. She had on one of those scoop neck T-shirts, wet down the front and baby blue, with sparkly letters saying *Nasty n' Nice*. She was glowing where Damon had rubbed with the rag.

He twirled around slow. 'Iceman,' he said low, 'you forget how to talk to a lady?'

'*Lady?!*' Leif was yelping again. 'Lady? Jesus Damon. You know her. You oughta know —'

Damon slipped off his barstool and stood close under Leif's swaying height. 'You got somethin you wanna say?'

Leif's eyes were rolling around in his head. 'Yah, yah —' He was choking almost, it sounded like his tongue had got loose and was swimming around in his mouth. 'I got somethin — you sonofa —'

he broke off, panting, with these little white bubbles in the corners of his lips.

Damon's eyes were just about shut. He was staring Leif down through the cracks. Leif's face was working hard, like he might start crying. Then Damon fixed his sites on me. 'Redbreast,' he said, 'get him outta here.'

'What'd you call her? What?'

I took hold of Leif's cut hand. 'C'mon.'

He didn't pull it away. Damon swung back to the bar and Joelle made like she was cleaning up. Leif came quietly. He followed me out of there like I was his mom.

I didn't have a dress. There was one from a wedding the summer before, but it bit in under my arms and anyway, it was pink. Maureen came into my room with something red laid over her arm. 'I got this that time your dad and me went to Vegas. Mutton dressed up for lamb.' She handed it over and sat down on the edge of my bed to light a smoke. 'Jesus Robin, you can't even see the floor in here.'

I slid the dress on over my head and it felt slippery going down. We were the same build and everything, even if she wasn't my real mom. I took a look in the mirror. It wasn't half bad.

Leif was feeling no pain when he picked me up. His breath ran over me where I held to his back and I could smell it, something sweet, maybe Comfort and Coke. I was getting used to the bike — leaning when he leaned, shaping my body to his back. The dress lifted and flew back from my legs.

The hall was hot, already crowded, and when I slipped off my jacket I could feel Leif looking, and other men too. My arms were bare. The dress was hugging up under my tits, making them feel special somehow, like they were something rare.

The band was setting up. We were too late for the dinner — the wives were all wrapping up scraps of lasagna and fried chicken and roast beef. There were dart boards down one of the walls and a crowd pairing up for mixed doubles. Leif ran his hand over my ass. 'Wait here,' he told me, and he made for the bar.

'Well fuck me.' Damon came out of nowhere. He was clean —his hair and beard slicked down. His eyes were all over me. 'Robin Redbreast. You got here just in time, you know that? I got no partner for this round.'

'Where's Joelle?'

'Her?' He jerked his head at the bathrooms. 'Pissed as a sailor's bitch.' Then he held his darts out to me like they were flowers. 'C'mon Redbreast, whaddayasay?'

' — I'm shitty at darts.'

'Hell no you're not.' He touched one of the tails to my collarbone, running it down to the dip in my neck. 'You're a natural.'

Leif was on his way back with a couple of rye and sevens tucked up against his chest. I watched his eyes land on the back of Damon's head, then jump away and start scanning for Joelle. Damon swivelled on the spot. 'Iceman,' he yelled out, 'get over here buddy!'

Leif came loping and held out my drink. 'Hey buddy.'

'I was just telling Robin here, we're startin up again an I got no partner.'

Leif lifted his glass and downed it. His mouth went dead all of a sudden, like he'd had a few cavities filled.

'C'mon Ice.' Damon was talking through his teeth. 'I'll keep her clean.'

Leif bent up the ends of his lips. 'Sure,' he said. 'Fill your boots.'

I couldn't miss. Damon's voice was in my ear and he was like Reveen — his clean black shirt and that wolf-man beard — I'd walk like a chicken if he told me, talk in tongues or sing opera while peeling off all my clothes. He stood beside me when it was my turn, his words warm in my head, telling me what to hit next.

'Twenties, Redbreast. Close the twenties. Seal 'er up.'

And I did. I'd just stare at a spot and flick, and smile when the tip drove in.

In between shots Damon handed me drinks or a drag off his smoke. The one time I looked round, Leif was helping Joelle out the side door. Her hair was all sweaty and her eyeshadow smeared. She was wearing Leif's body like a coat.

Thk. Thk. Thk. Two triples and a double bull. I won us the round. Damon lifted me in his hairy hands and spun, the dress flying out around us, then floating down easy when he slowed. He set me on my feet, dragging his knuckles over my tits and down.

'So that's what you been hidin in that mack.' There was something almost gentle in his voice. 'Who'da known?'

I looked deep into the pits of his eyes. 'You would,' I said.

'What?'

I reached down and lifted my dress, up over my thigh, the way he'd lifted the blanket that night. This look flashed over his face — fast — like a bird breaking cover for its life. I let the dress fall, then grabbed him by the collar of his shirt. He stumbled back when I kissed him, but I had hold of him by then.

Worst in the Back Field

Jessy's flat on her back in the hay, watching the slow swoop of a hawk through the rotted-out hole in the roof. Simon knows nothing about nothing, she thinks, and she jabs him in the ribs with her toe.

'Quit it,'
he says, but not like he means it. Not like he'll do a single damn thing if she doesn't.

In the red light of his eyelids, Simon is thinking: this barn is a head. Windows for eyes and a haychute ear — the other one cut off, like that painter in the soft brown book. The pictures move while you watch them — how? How, when he painted them yellow and blue way back when? But they do.

Sun heavy on Jessy's beginning breasts. She can feel them in the tight of her T-shirt, pushing up where Snoopy's ears have worn away. The shirt was bought big to grow into. Back then it flapped like a flag on her bird-bone chest — the cartoon dog dancing, flamenco black and red. Not now. Now she's bread dough, not bones. She can feel herself rising.

Skittering. Simon's eyes find the barnmouse,

crouched on a hay bale, smelling for traces of cat.
The mouse heart moving its fur. It's the same sil-
ver-brown as the barn.

    'Know what?'

says Jessy, and the mouse slips away through a crack.

    'The ravens came after our goats yesterday. Hey
    geek.

    Hey. SIMON!'

'Huh?'

    'I SAID, the ravens came after our goats.'

Simon sees a procession — the horned goats bleat-
ing, behind them, a black river of birds.

    'Dad got one with the shotgun. I know where
    he threw it. I'll take you there after.'

Ravens? He hardly ever sees them. Sometimes limp-
ing shadows by the dumpsters at school. Hunch-
backed and hopping. Or dark, dropping sounds in
the trees at the outskirts of town.

    'They're worst in the back field. They swoop
    down outta nowhere and eat the kids' eyes.'

    ' — No.'

    'Ask my dad.'

Simon covers his white face with the crook of his
arm.

What is he? thinks Jessy. She hikes up on her elbow
and stares at him, thin-skinned and silent, a pale
flower on the hay.

    'What are you,'

she says out loud,

    'an old lady or somethin?'

    'Shut up.'

    'You gonna make me?'

Silence. Haysticks in the soft backs of her knees.

Heat shoving splinters up under her skin. Jessy fills
up her lungs and yells,
   'JOHN JAY-COB JINKLEHEIMER
   SCHMIT!'
and flips like a woken-up dog, straight onto her
hands and knees. She shuffles to the broken-out
window, sits up on her heels and says,
   'Lookit.'

> Simon rolls onto his belly and crawls past her back,
> headed for the window further down. The barn
> groans like a doldrum boat. They look down from
> their stations, over the bobbing backs of scratching
> chickens, across the bright gravel to the garden, the
> sun-hat shadows their mothers cast. Jessy's mom talks
> with her hands. She points at her plants, stoops down
> to snatch yellowed leaves and crush beetles between
> her nails. Then his own mother. Trailing behind.
> Caressing the tomato plants. Straightening and
> smelling her fingers.

Jessy's lips move in sync with her mother's.
   'I can't get over how much sun we're having.
   Just look at my PEPPERS!'
The voice comes out perfect, like it's been squat-
ting on the back of her tongue. She spits on what's
left of the window. Watches it slip down the glass.

> I am in one eye, thinks Simon, and Jessy is in the
> other. We are the pupils. Jessy claps her hands in his
> ear, clap CLAP. She looms over him, the braid swing-
> ing down from her shoulder, woven brown like a
> rope in his face.
>   'Wanna see something?'

She takes hold of his hand, and it folds up like silk
in her palm. She pulls him to the pile of old crates
in the corner. Kept for kindling, she thinks. Kept
for burning but left here to rot.

> He follows like a kite, caught up in the shapes the
> crates paint on the silvery walls — ribcages, spiders,
> a lightening-torn tree.

Jessy holds a finger to her lips. She crouches, and
Simon kneels lightly beside her. In the mouth of an
overturned crate, Smoke lies on her side, suckling
her still-blind litter. The black runt pulls free and
turns its face their way. The ears still flat from
birthing, the mouth and nose all rosy red.

> Simon re-opens the thought like a book — we're
> inside a big head. The grey cat and its kittens are
> ideas in the brain of the loft. His eyes follow the slat
> pile to the rafters, where the barn swallows build
> their mud huts.

He's not looking, thinks Jessy, and her arm rockets
out like a crossbow, knocking him flat on his back.

> 'Hey!'
> Simon cries out, but she's kicked up the trapdoor
> and dropped out of sight.

She skips the last rungs and hits the ground running, rams the barn door and shoots into the yard.
On the far porch their fathers sit forward and wave —
slow motion with wide, stupid smiles, like the men

88

in the May Day parade. She blows them a kiss and
tears into the field like a fire.

>Simon wavers in the yawning barn door. I will sit
>with the grown-ups, he thinks. But finds himself
>following the white back of her T-shirt. He walks
>slowly at first, then breaks into a stumbling run.

Over the rise, Jessy kneels in the high grass. She fits
a green blade between her thumbs and blows until
it buzzes and screams. Simon appears on the hori-
zon, and she fights the desire to jump up like a dog
at a doorknock.
   'HA HA!'
she yells,
   'Simon runs like a gi–irl!'

>He walks the last little way, gasping to catch hold of
>his breath. Jessy glares at his new runners, then tilts
>the plane of her face and fixes him in a stare. In
>place of her eyes, two beetles lie on their backs,
>lashing their tiny black legs.

   'What're you wearin shoes for?'
   'Huh?'
She yanks the tails of his shoelace bows.
   'Take em off.'
   'What? — Why?'
   'WHY? Because it feels good, stupid.'
She rips the grassblade down its seam.
   'Because I say so, that's why.'
Simon shifts on his feet. He glances back over his
shoulder toward the house.
   'Chickenshit.'

'Am not.'
' — Well?'
His forehead falls like a curtain. He drops to one
knee and struggles with his shoes and socks.
'Leave 'em there. We'll get 'em on the way back.'
She springs up and snatches his hand.

> Simon drags like a plow, turning up rocks with his
> soft white soles. His fingers hitched in hers. She
> tramples the high grass, her feet farm-sure and the
> braid like a whip in her wake.

She rears up at the old fence and throws down his
hand. A stand of birch saplings marks the edge of
the woods. She lifts up her finger and points.
'There. You see it?'

> He does. By the white foot of a tree lies a glossy
> black hump. One wing outstretched, the feathertips
> open. Blood like a paintstroke where it hit the pale
> bark and slid down.

Jessy swings up onto the fence.
'You comin?'
She drops down on the far side.

> Simon looks past her to the raven. His shoulders
> fall and he turns, first his face, then the delicate bones
> of his back. He takes three steps away, then stops
> and whirls suddenly, hurling himself at the fence.
> Half-way over, his brain goes blank. He lets go with
> his hands and straightens up tall on the fencerail.
> Smiles like an acrobat and falls.

T H E   H U N T E R

'YOU'RE NOT TO set foot in those woods.'

Not set foot?

Not a small bare foot in the pine grove, pitch on your soles and the underboughs stroking you sweet and green? A running-shoe foot, blue in the birch leaves, flat yellow arrowheads carved by the skeleton trees. A rubber boot foot. A black rubber boot in the swamp — the slippery log bridge to its wet brown heart, frogs diving deep in their skins or singing or pushing out delicate strings of eggs. The sighing swamp. Cattails hung heavy with blackbirds, fox flashing in the brush, and weasel and skunk, and the skunk cabbage flowering like fire —

'You're not to set foot.'

But it's a shortcut. Half the distance of the scooping school road, grey through the houses and flat as a snake hammered flat on a rock. That wasn't you. You didn't touch it even, you only watched — the forked tongue flicking and the hammer and the boy's bloody hand gone limp. The school road's dead, as dead as the woods are alive. You cut free from the road just as soon as the house can't see — the windows your mother's eyes, her wooden-house head, you coming and going through her teeth.

The school path is simple, brown and well worn, a diagonal stroke through the trees to the goalposts at the end of the field. It's the path your feet know best, but there are others — the swamp path, the clearing path, the creek path, the reserve path. *The reserve path*. Criss-crossed with trip roots, twisting and falling away down the hill. Down to the bottom — the shacks piled up like a landslide, splinter doors and everyone outside when it's any way warm, outside stoves cut from oil barrels, outside tables that were powerline spools. The same powerlines humming high overhead, passing over but not dropping down. And the dogs. *Reserve dogs*, said in the same voice as *wolf* or *bear*, but louder, like you only need fear them half-way. You can shoot reserve dogs, and people do — one on its side in the slough, blood like a bandanna on its neck, and that hawk on the fencepost staring down. Or at the dump, a dog leg sticking out from under an old armchair, a paw like the paw on your dog at home, only nothing like your dog, fat toffee brown and tied up in the yard, with its tail drawing fans in the leaves.

Reserve dogs are silver, black patches or white, fur falling out in clumps, sharp noses, bare teeth, standing stiff in the wind on the hillside above the reserve. Six at least, sometimes more. Sometimes a forest of dogs, more than you can count before you turn a half circle and run. They can smell you if you're not down wind. They can hide in the woods, hide their thin silver legs, silver ribs in the sapling birch stands.

But it's more than the dogs. You can see a dog attack, name it, horrify yourself with the thought of your small hands pulled off like mittens, tossed and torn in their glittering teeth. The other is different. You have no picture for it, only a dark hole — things whispered, woods forbidden, stories sung on the flat grey platter of the schoolyard. *Indians.* There was the girl they dragged into the bushes and — what? What girl? Scalpings. People painted with honey, painted with blood, tied to anthills or to one of those trees where the bears come to scratch. White babies, carried by reserve dogs, not eaten or even bitten, but carried, back to the oil barrel stoves, stuck through with a skewer and turned on a spit until they go brown, as brown as little Indian babies. Whose babies? Whose? Arrows from nowhere. Silent brown feet and snares, animal gods and tomahawks flipping end over blade through the air.

Still, the reserve path beckons, and you find yourself shimmying

down the hill to crouch in a thicket of snowberries, down wind of
the dogs. The Indians aren't afraid of their dogs, not even the babies,
set down on a broken fridge, or on a blanket in the dirt, or tied to
their mothers like they were bandaged there. The children throwing
sticks to their dogs — thin as sticks themselves, ribs in their skin like
dog ribs in mottled fur. The boys naked to the waist in summer,
strong as white boys twice their size, dangerous in their desks at the
back of the class, or not in their desks, not anywhere to be found.
The girls in their braids, more often in school, rubber boots too big
in winter, like cows in the hallway, shuffling with their heads bent
low. At recess they line along the cement block wall, lips moving
gently, so quiet no white child can hear. At the lunch bell they're
gone, slipping away down the hill to the shacks their mothers wait
in — to eat what? White bread from a rectangle loaf? Weak soup
from a can? Or the leg of a rabbit, caught in a snare or shot by a
brother or father, by an Indian hunter in the woods.

You see one once. You're lying on your belly in the fox grass
when he steps out from the trees, a green velvet curtain and the
magic show starting — him the magician, soft rabbits and birds on
his belt, blood bright on the thighs of his jeans. Not animals from a
hat. No black satin top hat and white-tipped stick and white rabbit
kicking like mad. Not like Munro the Magnificent at the fair — the
rabbit's pink eyes and the pink insides of its ears crushed tight in
Munro's gloved fist. The Indian's rabbits are dead, soft grey and his
birds are brown — not doves fluttering up like lost white souls, but
dead, dark brown and peaceful as the ground, beating his thighs like
a drum. He appears from the green past, his hair a black river behind
him, his feet lost in the whiskery grass, like he's grown up from the
earth in a mist. Even in blue jeans and a mack he's a true Indian, the
kind you dream of. The animals slung low on his hips, the weight of
them making him sacred. You lay there on your belly, like somebody
praying, long after he's gone.

You look for him. See traces in the silent brown boys, the girls
twisting their feet like they're caught in traps, rearing at the sound

of the bell, suddenly graceful, taking light strong strides over the field and leaping away down the hill. It's in the women — a red-brown light in the mothers, smoking on overturned crates, bending in thin cotton prints, in slippers or boots, bending to slide wood into the stove, or to lift a child, or a never-white undershirt from the bucket to hang on a length of hairy twine. Or the old men — up to their knees in the river, lines trailing in the river's pull, out past the traintracks and the tires, never hooting when something bites, just the slow secret smile when the fat fish glints in their hands. The young men swinging axes into wood, or standing back to roll cigarettes and look up at the sky. Naked to the waist like the boys, scars on their backs and eagles tattooed on their chests. And their hair, more beautiful than any woman's. Black as the jackpine ravens. Black as the glimmering river's floor.

You look for him in town. The men lined up down the liquor store wall, waiting for the sign to flip and the bar to slide back from the door. You've never been inside, but you can see it — the man with white sleeves rolled and gold on his finger, punching the number buttons, filling the drawer with their crumpled up bills and their coins. The drawer shooting open, the bell ringing for every Indian, every single sale.

You pass there on Saturdays, but somehow you know it's the same every day, except Sunday, when the liquor store's closed, and your mother and father sit singing in the hard-backed pews, and you break stale cookies and swallow juice in the jesus-postered basement below the priest's creaking back-and-forth feet. On Sundays the Indians must sleep, but you pass them on Saturdays, sitting beside your mother in her long brown car. Men like piles of leaves — you could jump in them, brown leaves piled up against the sunlit brick. Sometimes a woman. Sometimes in winter, the overhang icicles grazing the tops of their heads.

You keep watch at the Tomboy. Your mother wheeling her cart through the aisles, pulling down red boxes of cereal, dropping apples in a bag, grabbing the same laundry soap, the same sweet softener smell. And you — supposed to be choosing a comic but pressed to the window instead, handprints, noseprint on the glass, watching a man in the parking lot, a man like a tower, a towering Indian, watching him stagger through the cars with a bottle in his hand, the cleaner your mother uses at home, skull and crossbones under the sink, never touch it, let alone drink. He lifts it to his lips. Three steps closer to your car and you watch, not breathing as he crashes against it, cleaner splashing on the hood, the car shaking as he reaches a hand out to steady himself, his huge brown hand on the hood of your car. Two men in red and white candy shirts come running with brooms and chase him, sweep him into the street like a dog.

They sold him that stuff. You know that much. This is the grocery store, where your mother buys cleaners of all kinds. Is he trying to clean something? Something inside — make it hard as a toilet or a sink, sparkly white and smelling like nothing that was ever alive? Alive like his hand. You're too far away to make out the raw knuckles, the black bruise of a bad tattoo and the thumbnail torn away. You see only the shape — a bird's wing sewn to his body, brown feather fingers folding the bottle to his chest.

You keep looking. At the bus depot there's a parcel from your grandparents far away, grey-haired sweets and sweaters never really wool. Your father's blunt back at the desk and you at the window again, watching Indian girls, older sisters of the ones in school, lined up leaning on the glass. It's not even dark yet, but a green car slides up like a serpent, and the first one steps down off the curb — black lattered nylons and a dirty white dress — she steps down off the curb like a sleepwalker and folds into the open-mouth door.

You see Indians wherever you go. Sometimes only shadows — girl shapes on the hill, boy shapes in the woods, pulling frogs from the water, red berries from bushes, white mushrooms from tree stumps, brown birds from the sky. You see them in the past, the present, the future. You see them in classrooms, on busses or in malls, long after you've learned to say Natives, Aboriginals, First Nations. You fear them. You fear them, yet you find yourself watching, unable to turn away. And always you remember the hunter — his black hair dancing, his drumming thighs, his low-slung belt of death, and life.

E V O L U T I O N

'WHITETIP ISLAND?' LEN bounced a fist off the cross-stitched cushion beside him. 'It's a goddamn paradise!'

Kitty-corner on the sectional, Marion sighed long and low. 'Keith hates going anywhere.' She nibbled a hangnail. 'We haven't set a pinky toe out of the city since the family reunion, and that's six years ago now, I remember, I was eight months gone with Kerri-Lynn.'

Keith reached a hairy hand down to rearrange his balls. 'Somebody get her a violin, willya?'

'Now I'm serious.' Len swung his pink face from Keith to Marion, Marion to Keith. 'You two lovebirds oughta go.' He waggled a fat finger. 'It's a goddamn paradise. Tell 'em Lou.'

Louise glanced up from a dark stream of coffee. She set the silver pot down softly and lifted the cake knife, holding it poised over lumpy red strawberries and swirls of cream. 'Oh, it's a paradise alright.' She narrowed the black mess of her lashes. The blade flashed in her hand and she let fly, driving it deep into the heart of the shortcake. 'And we all know what happened in paradise.'

Silence. Len wiped the grin off his lips. Marion froze, then quivered a little, like a bloodhound. Keith shot smoke out his nose and leaned forward to grind out the butt.

'It all started on our third night there.' Louise shovelled out helpings and handed them round. 'There was this Australian couple at our table, Marv and Sally Putnam. Oh, we took to him right off the bat — he was a big handsome guy, sold real estate down there in Sydney.' She reached a finger up under her jawbone, feeling the loose skin for a pulse. 'God knows what he was doing with her. She barely said two words all night, just sat there staring with these pinhole eyes.'

Len sucked up his last strawberry and let out a small, wet burp.

'Now I know love is blind,' Louise went on, 'but this one — she had the widest mouth you ever laid eyes on, and more than her fair share of teeth. Skin like a glass of skim milk. Imagine, in all that sun. So white it was blue. Her hair too. She could've been one of those albinos, you know, if it wasn't for the dark little eyes.' She did a little shiver. 'It gave you the creeps just looking at her. How she ever hooked a catch like him —'

> *They ran from him like crabs. Marv was like a wave the first time I saw him, thundering down the field with the ball curled into his chest. All through the stands the students chanted Marvellous Marv, Marvellous Marv. I saw myself caught in that wave, carried the green distance with everything washed from my path. I paced along the wire mesh fence. My hair was piled up high and white — it caught the light, it wasn't long before I caught his eye.*

'Opposites attract.' Marion wafted Keith a look. 'That's what they say.'

Keith pitched back in the Lazy-Boy. 'Attack,' he corrected her. 'Opposites attack.'

Louise ignored them. 'We all had a few drinks, you know how it goes on vacation.'

'Not really,' Marion sighed.

'Not really,' Keith whined. 'Not reeeeeally.'

Len heaved up out of the pillows. 'No holds barred on that island, buddy.' He made for the liquor cabinet, winking over his shoulder at Keith. 'Speaking of the beast, what say we kickstart this coffee?'

Keith's lip curled up in a smile. 'Does the Pope shit in the woods?'

Marion shook her head. 'Oh Keith.'

Len twisted the cap off the Black Velvet. 'Marion?'

'Oh I don't know, after all that wine —'

'She's a cheap date.' Keith sucked his middle finger. 'Aren't ya honey?'

Marion's face puckered. Len christened everyone's cup and lumbered back to his corner, parking the bottle close by.

'As I was saying,' said Louise.

Len sniggered. 'Before she was so rudely interrupted —'

Louise shut him up with a look. 'As I was saying. We all got a little tipsy. Marv kept telling these hilarious stories. We were all killing ourselves — all of us but her, I should say. About the only time she made a peep was when she excused herself to go out to the toilet huts. We didn't think too much about it then, but she was gone for a long time. Not only that, but when she finally came back, one of the bartenders came in right after.' She stroked a crumb from the lap of her slacks. 'He was soaking wet too. Wearing the skimpiest Speedo you ever saw. What was his name, Len?'

'Barney.'

'That's right, Benny. A great big muscly black with hair out to here. Oh, he was friendly enough, but not the type you trust — if you take my meaning.'

Len topped up his cup. 'A damn fine bartender, mind you. A real whiz with a pina colada.'

The sand was shifting under my feet and the moon was full, hanging low in the sky, like the only fruit left on the tree. He came up from the sea, a dark man parting the waves, in one hand a speargun, in the other, three glittering fish. I lost my footing. Drunk, I fell forward onto the beach. His voice swam out of the

darkness, What you doing Sally Putnam? You
swimmin in the sand?

Louise made a move for Keith's cigarettes. 'You mind?'

He flipped open the pack. 'So. Little Sally was getting it. Do do that voo-doo.'

'Oh Keith,' Marion moaned.

'Oh Keith what?' He turned on her. 'Everybody knows blacks get it up for blondes. It's a fact.'

Marion gasped. Len snorted and hauled up for a round with the bottle.

'Just wait now.' Louise was glimmering in the flick of the lighter. 'Just you wait. We made plans to go snorkelling with them in the morning. I guess Marv was used to her silent act. He just put his arm around her and said something lovey-dovey every once in a while. But you should've seen how she looked at that arm. Like she was doing him a favour to let him keep it there. Like what she really wanted to do was — I don't know — bite it.'

Keith flicked open a shirt button and scratched his matted chest. 'Kinky.'

'Not that kind of bite.' Louise took a long, hollow-cheeked drag. 'It turned out they had a couple of kids back in Sydney, both boys. But you couldn't picture her being a mother, not in a million years. She just wouldn't have the instinct.'

Marion giggled out of the blue. 'Instinct,' she whispered. Her cheeks were starting to blotch up.

Louise lost her thread and looked over at Len, who said, 'Snorkelling,' into his cup.

'Right. Only we didn't end up going. I woke up with one of my migraines, so Len went over to tell them we'd try again the next day. Marv already had all the stuff rented, so he said they'd go anyways, you know, scout out the best spots. When we met up with him later on at the bar he was solo. Sally's lying down, he told us, she crossed paths with a shark.'

*The water was shallow over the reef, but it dropped
down twenty feet at the edge and turned a terrible
shade of blue. I reached the ledge long before Marv —
I could hear him calling after me to wait, his voice
riding the breeze like the bark of a dog. I dove, swam
out a few strokes and floated, watching my shadow
fold into the ocean floor. The shark came round a finger of the reef, as sudden and silver as a ghost. Its
prehistoric eye met mine and something twisted in my
chest, a violent, wriggling twist like a fish on the floor
of a boat. A gliding moment more and then it turned,
a bright unfolding curve and it was gone. I hung in
the sea with the reef like a cliff at my back, until Marv
closed his hand round my wrist.*

'Marv told that bartender Benny,' Len jumped in. 'My wife saw a
shark today, he says, and Benny tells him, No shark here Mistah
Putnam. So Marv says, I'm telling you mate, she saw a shark, out at
the edge of the reef, round back where our bungalow is, a six-footer
she said. So Benny laughs like Marv told him a great joke. Six-
footer, he says, that not a shark. That a fish.'

'Pppp — haaawwwww!' Marion sprayed spit down Louise's sleeve.
Keith grunted. 'Uppity sonofabitch.'

*It wasn't the first I'd seen. That day at Cronulla with
Mother and Dad, a tiger shark cut through the crowd
of bathers and took a small boy. Dad threw me over
his shoulder and everyone thundered for shore. There
were those with their thighs scraped raw where the
shark's abrasive sides had brushed them by. Dad told
me later the boy had eaten kippers for lunch. A shark
can smell that Sally. The devils can smell right through
you.*

Louise stubbed her cigarette and hooked into the pack for another. 'That night Marv got really loaded. The band came on and some-body got hold of a broomstick so we could all do the limbo. When it got to Marv's turn he went down so low he fell flat on his back in the sand. For a second it looked like he had the wind knocked out of him, but then all of a sudden he cracked up laughing. Of course that got everybody going. He looked pretty funny down there, with the shirt up around his neck and his face going scarlet. You never saw anybody laugh so hard — and he wouldn't quit either. Even after the rest of us settled down. Even after the band quit playing and everybody was just standing there, staring. Me and Len got down on our knees beside him, you know, tried to calm him down, but it was like he couldn't hear us. He was shaking all over, laughing so hard there were tears running down his face. We were starting to wonder, you know, if maybe we should get some help.'

Len shook his head. 'Then out of the blue he sits up and looks around like the alarm clock just went off. I'm right mates, he says, no fear.'

Keith stuck his cup out for a fill-up. 'Sounds like a faggot.'

'Oh Keith,' Marion wailed, her eyes all boggy.

'Oh Keith oh Keith oh Keith,' Keith panted. 'You gettin off yet Marion?'

Marion's mouth fell open like an old flower. She bit down hard on her wobbly lip.

'Len and me walked him back to their bungalow.' Louise was staring at the coffee pot, addressing the warped reflection in its side. 'We weren't too sure if he'd make it on his own. It was sad really — at the door he wanted us to come in, kept saying how he didn't want to be alone. Don't be a silly goose, Marv, I told him. Sally's in there, and she's probably sound asleep. Now you be a good boy and don't wake her up. But we felt terrible, didn't we Len, just leaving him there.'

Marv felt his way through the darkness, stumbling on the cases and crumpling into bed. I rose quietly and left. All down the path, the palm fronds glistened like broad black hands. At the beach the breeze lifted my nightie, drew it over my head, let it drop like a skin. I lay down on my back, clawing the sand, lifting handfuls to sift down my thighs, my belly, my breasts. I closed my eyes and the sand pooled in their sockets. His voice swam out of the blackness, What you doing Sally Putnam? His laugh like the lap of the sea.

Louise bowed her head, remembering. 'We took the long way back to our bungalow, around the beach instead of down the path.'

'Creepy-crawlies in those palms,' said Len. 'Lizards popping up like prairie dogs, I kid you not. Beetles this big.' He held up a fist, and Marion squealed and shuddered all over.

'We were almost all the way back to our bungalow when it hit me that I'd lost my purse. You know how you lose track after a few drinks.'

'Sure.' Keith licked his chops. 'That's how Marion here lost her cherry.'

Marion gagged on her drink. She turned pink and coughed up into her napkin.

Len beamed and lifted his cup. 'Gesundheit!'

'So — we turned around and headed back.' Louise's voice crept down into her bosom. 'There was a full moon, so we could see our footprints in the sand. We came around a clump of trees not too far from the path to their bungalow, and sure enough, there was my purse, lying open with everything spilled out on the sand. That's when Len put his hand over my mouth and pointed.' Her finger rose up, pointing past them, deep into the shadowy drapes. 'There they were. No more than a stone's throw from our noses. Naked as the day they were born and going at it like a couple of ferrets.'

Marion yelped.

'Let me guess.' Keith grinned, lighting up with difficulty. 'A big black on a little bitty blonde.'

Len saluted him. 'Right again buddy, right a-goddamn-gain.'

Marion stuck her finger in the melty red cream that was slithering down the side of the shortcake. 'Sally and Benny? — Right out in the open?'

'That's right. Right out in the open.' Louise tore off a chunk of spongecake and shoved it in her mouth. 'Needless to say, we stuffed everything back in that purse and got out of there lickety-split. Of course we were still supposed to go snorkelling with them in the morning. I didn't want to go, but Len said we had to. I mean what are you going to say?'

'Hey buddy,' Keith roared, 'the bartender's nailing your wife!'

'Well that's it,' said Louise, 'that's just it. So we went. Marv wasn't looking too rough, considering the shape he was in the night before. You wouldn't know what she'd been up to either. She was her usual self, all glassy eyes and letting everyone else do the talking. Marv figured we better keep over the reef, since Sally saw the shark out where it got deep. We weren't out there long when we heard him yelling, so we stood up to see what was going on. He was calling after Sally, but she was way ahead of him, headed straight out for the ledge. He took off after her, but she had a good lead. She reached the line where the water turned dark and stood up with her back to us. Then she dove in. Marv crashed out to where she went down and stuck his face in the water. After a few seconds he turned and yelled for us to get help. We got back to the beach as fast as we could, and Len ran down the path to the bar, and I stood there and watched Marv dive down and come up over and over. You can bet I was watching for shark fins too.'

Len cleared the creamy phlegm in his throat. 'I came round with them in the boat, Benny and a couple of the other natives. It had a glass bottom in it, so you could see what all was underneath.' He knocked back the dregs in his cup. 'As soon as we get out to where

Marv is, me and Benny haul him on board, and then Benny dives in. Marv's watching over the side, and me and the others are watching through the bottom, but there's no sign of her. All we can see is Benny swimming back and forth, swimming circles like a goddamn black dolphin or something. After a half hour or so, Benny climbs back in the boat. He looks Marv dead in the eye and says, She gone now Mistah Putnam. Then he reaches down to start up the engine.'

Marion snuffled into her napkin. Keith took the Black Velvet by the neck and found out it was empty.

'They never found a trace of her,' Louise murmured, 'not a trace. Oh, everybody had it worked out one way or another. Some said it was a shark, or else one of those poisonous sea snakes. Some figured she got sucked out in a current. Of course me and Len never breathed a word. But with all we knew — well — we had to wonder.'

> *The shark was where I knew it'd be. I dove down and took hold of its fin, and it broke for the deep like a great white horse. The skin wore away from my arms where I held to its back. The water turned black. Teeth cut my gums, my throat split open in slits, and the fin thrust up through the flesh of my back like a sword. The sea was trembling. I swung my head from side to side, caught a scent of blood and turned.*

A REAL PRESENT

Up the front of the bus there's an old man dozing. He's several seats away but I can smell the liquor in his body, like liquor soaked up in a rag and left in the sink, turning sour and sad.

I can smell him as if he's close enough to tell me a secret.

As if I'm sitting on his knee.

Roy Philipchuk was so good to us.

He was the first in that Alberta town to welcome us when we came from across the sea, my parents with their strange voices, like Brits lying on their backs and yawning. Their stories of the sun, the sharks and the kangaroos. And their two small children.

Roy was so good to us — helped us find a house and fill it with furniture, sold my parents his old Ford pick-up for too cheap, told us now we had a truck we could come out to his cabin on the lake. And we did, my brother and me riding in back, our noses to the wind, happy like dogs.

Roy was so good to us on those afternoons, gave us white bread with strawberry jam and kool-aid the colour of flowers. We stuffed ourselves, my brother and I, and my parents drank beer with Roy — though he had three to their one — and we all lay looking up, surrounded by trees so tall, water so dark, and flies as fat as the fat berries that grew wild in the brush, the ones we had to learn names for. There were no deadly spiders anymore, only ones that gave welts.

And welts were good for getting love.

My father was the first to try water-skiing, his face hitting the water again and again — he had to be Canadian, more Canadian than Roy, or even Roy's two sons, who piloted the boat like gods, with the sun in their limbs and beer in their hands. I remember loving one of them — his wind-swept hair at the helm of the boat, his cruel smile — but it can't be true. I was only six.

My father learned in time. He and Roy's two sons tore up the lake's back like men with whips, while Roy sat drinking in the shade, while I played with my brother in the underdock shadow and slime. My mother watched us all from the shallows, closing her fingers round the drowning roots of a birch, the one that grew too close to the lake.

Later, the men would build a fire, and Roy would send my brother and I for sticks, *Green ones, mind, or they'll catch and burn.* We'd have contests to see who could get their marshmallow the brownest without setting it alight, but mine always caught in the end. I couldn't keep far enough from the flame.

Later still, the mosquitos came, and then the dark. Roy would kick at a beer can with his boot — heavy farming boots he wore no matter what the heat — he'd kick at a can until it rolled away into the blackness, and then he'd ask me to sit on his knee.

Even though my parents were right there, I felt afraid of his hand — his callused, old man's hand on my skin turned golden and amphibious by the lake. His sad, sugary breath. The smell of hops and loneliness in my face.

The bus lurches, the old man lifts his head and looks at me, but my eyes slip away like foxes to the hole in my jeans.

I wish this bus ride were done.

The only reason I ever take the number eleven to this suburb, to the end of the earth, is to see my father. And his wife. In their new house that my father's fixing up and getting just right.

When we all still lived together, the four of us in that small Alberta town, my father fixed up our house until it was a dream. A dream any woman would've died for. Any woman except my mother.

A couple of months ago she and I were looking through pictures of that life, the life before I turned ten and we came to the coast and split apart. We found frame after frame of that house, documented, the best a man could do. Cedar shingles like feathers outside and everything warm and lovely within — stained glass, wood and plants. In the yard two cats, two dogs, a treehouse with a swing. All by his hand. *Look at that house*, my mother said, holding out a photo, *it's perfect*.

The pictures of that life had been locked away in a trunk, left with my mother because my father couldn't bear the pain. No one had looked at them for a dozen years, as though the four of us were partners in a heinous crime, that none would mention and all hoped to forget.

I was surprised at how well I remembered things — the layout of that cedar house, the garden I weeded with my brother, the cats, both dead of distemper, the dogs, one left with Roy at the lake because it barked too much, one brought along, kept by my father in the split, a flesh and fur memory of their life. I remembered everything right. My mother like a mermaid, braided hair touching the lake alongside her golden arms. My father with a wilder beard, crouched by the fire with smoke in his eyes and an arm around his small son. And me on old Roy's lap, his eyes half shut with drink, his hard hot hand on my knee.

The old man's whispering sad secrets to his chest, reminding me of the last time I came out this way. My father drank one beer after another, as though the bottles were tied to a long, invisible thread. By the time we'd finished our ice cream, he was ready to cry about my mother. He looked into his empty bowl and told me he'd never love another like her — she was the one he'd had his children with, she was the one who knew him for what he really was. No, he'd never love another like her, and his wife made noise in the kitchen, clattering the plates into the dishwasher, banging the pots in the sink so she couldn't hear.

The bus doors sigh. The old man lumbers down the steps and I watch his broad, bewildered face through the glass, the face of a dog left off at the side of the road. I try to imagine he's going to his daughter's house. She'll be angry he's drunk, but she'll give him something to eat and put him to bed all the same.

Tonight it's my father's birthday, so maybe he'll be in better spirits.

Or maybe he'll have an excuse to drink even more.

In any case, I've brought a real present, the first real one in years. It's a wooden frame with six spaces. I've chosen and pasted six photos with care — three of myself, two of my brother, one of my father and the two of us, standing at the edge of Roy's lake. All taken before the split. None of my mother, though she's there in all of them, like a shadow. Now matter how drunk he gets, I'll tell him, *Look, there we were. And here we are now.*

No Stone on the Grave

CAROL'S HOUSE IS where we play. It's the same on both floors, so you forget where you are, and you have to look up from your Barbies to remember the living room up there, or the rec room beneath your bent knees. Both have a couch staring out the long window. Both have leaning chairs and a wood TV and the black of a fireplace gaping. It's a modern house. Carol and I creep around the inside like mice in a bakery cake.

The yard's a long basin, sloped on all sides so you can run end to end like a marble in a bowl. Only there's one corner where we never run — the corner where a perfect white boulder rises up from the ground. Troll boulder, we call it, though never in earshot of the brown cake house.

Carol's mother is a troll.

Her father's a scarecrow, straw sticking out from his ribs, out in the yard, high rubber boots and a rake in his hand. He smiles all the time, a quarter-moon smile on his burlap bag face, his collar done drawstring tight. We love him, but not Carol's mother. Her mother's a troll.

Her brother's a monster in the cage of his room. We sneak in when he's out, open magazines to find women with hair fanned, black hair like horse flanks, or cornsilk pale. Women laid back on red satin sheets, eyes like dog eyes — the dog when you haven't walked it, lying on the blanket looking up. Their breasts are balloons with a darker pink knot, a belly button before it sinks in. Carol and me on our knees, women flat in our flipping hands, legs falling open to show us the dark, secret gash. We laugh ourselves sick in the smell of her big brother's room, the walls covered with men, mesh masks and helmets, hockey sticks bent in their hands.

The troll must know. She'd find those magazines with the snout of her vacuum, sucking her son's dirt the way she sucks dirt from every corner of the house, digging a path through his animal briefs, feeling up under the bedspread to the ragged brown lip of the box. She hauls the poor vacuum by the scruff of its neck — a zoo keeper in her olive green blouse, face grim, rubber gloves like bird feet, so bright. Dim clothes, dusky skin and hair boot black, standing up on her head like a hedge.

There's a hedge around the yard, waist-high, troll glove yellow when it blooms. The scarecrow keeps it trim, clipping carefully, creeping sideways like a slow insect feeding. He reaches the end and looks down on the troll's behind, brown slacks sticking up from the pansy bed. He waits until she swivels her head — all fours in the dirt, saying too low there, there uneven, do it again.

The house is rung round with pansies, each plant separate in the dirt. At the front and back doors the huge-blooming peonies, raw pink and obscene — any head that droops down gets snipped off by the troll's scissors and floated on the table in a bowl. We call them peenies, for the soft dangling secrets so silly on boys, so wrinkled and red-heavy on men. We're thrilled when boys threaten with their flies, but when they finally show us, it's sad. No wonder only wild boys kick there — an older boy on his side in the schoolyard, blue as a baby born wrong.

The troll had one. Carol doesn't know how she knows it, but she does. A blue baby. Dead in her arms and buried with no stone on the grave.

She's a troll.

Carol catches her sleeve on the brown plastic jug, the swollen bag flying, milk arcing from its cut-open spout. She panics, catching it and squeezing, screaming as it paints like a spraygun, the shining stove, the long counter, milk clouding the spotless brown tile. The troll grabs her arm. She twists — her hand the dark mouth of a dog, Carol wailing and me backing into the hall. Carol screams and cries and finally falls silent with the fingers still biting her arm. An Indian burn, like the mean boys at school, only longer and harder and worse. She wears the red twist like a band on her arm, and the next day, pansy-dark, troll fingerprints deep in her skin.

The troll shows her teeth when, ever so rarely, she tips her blunt head back and laughs. Never at anything we say. Once in the kitchen, a man on the radio, speaking the liquidy tangle of language she knew as a child. Once when she doesn't know we're nearby, playing spies in the long yellow hedge. It's something the scarecrow says. He's taking his chances on a spring day, stooping down to plant words in her ear. It's a miracle, for something that hard to crack — a rock splitting open, her laughter falling red on the lawn.

Carol's loose teeth are never left to fall out. She hides them, but the troll always checks, forcing her brown fingers through Carol's soft lips, counting along until one of them wiggles and gives way. She doesn't use string. No knot tied to the doorknob, or like the Wesechko kids — all seven with their teeth tied to the bumper of their father's truck, pulling everything rotten or loose in one go. Horrible, but somehow not nearly so bad as the troll's clamping finger and thumb. Carol's head back like a horse head, her eye rolling and wild, and that hand in her mouth — wiggle, pause, wiggle — as if she's speaking to the tooth, asking it how brutal she should be. One yank is all it ever takes, the tooth white and jagged, Carol's head falling, face crumpling, blood threading from the corners of her lips. The tooth fairy won't come. The troll keeps Carol's teeth, along with the monster's, in a red wooden matchbox in the cupboard high over the fridge. She climbs her low ladder and stands there like she can't see us, reaching for the matchbox and shaking it close to her ear.

We hear bats in the cake house, chattering in the hollow walls. The chimney's an up-and-down tunnel, from the roof to the rec room, where we lie on the carpet, stringing yellow and green plastic beads. A sickening thump. The bat struggles from the fire grate, hooked wings in the carpet and it's crawling, hauling its black body our way. We're frozen, stretched out on our bellies and screaming like seals. The bat squeals. The troll thunders into the room, her broom held high. Three feet from our faces, she swings down on the bat's head, cracking it like a hairy black egg. She shovels it up in her dustpan. Sprinkles salt on the spreading red stain.

The scarecrow isn't there. He's never there when things happen — either at work in his brown office, or out in yard, sprinkling white weed killer and watering, walking long swathing lines, like knitting a green sweater, the gas mower the most noise he ever makes.

In winter he wets the snow with his hose, lets its freeze and then wets it again. We skate the length of the sunken yard, and other kids come, and Carol — baby fat with her father's painted smile, horse-loving and normally unseen — Carol's the queen of the yard. The troll watches from the window, cleaning the wide pane with a bottle of anti-freeze blue. She watches us wheeling in our snowsuits, her husband and his hose, a child among children, despite his straw height. More than anything, she watches the far corner of the yard, where the white globe rises up from the snow. It should be a snow-ball, the first stage of a snowman, rolled up by the children to the tops of our heads. But it's not. It belongs to the troll, rock solid, white summer and winter alike.

It's shiny, coated with bright, stinking oil paint four times a year. She paints it at the turn of each season, circling, climbing her three-step ladder to get the top right, just right, perfect white. A rock like nature never made, a shape seen rolling off cartoon cliffs and nowhere else. She must've ordered it that way. One day, before Carol can remember, she must've ordered it, had it delivered, like a desk or a bed, or a crib.

Was it bare? The monster might remember — was it naked when it first rolled over the lawn, only the shape of it strange, the colour still natural rock? Did she paint the first coat? We could ask him, if we ever asked him anything. If he was ever in the house without the lock on his bedroom door.

We could ask the scarecrow, if he ever remembered a thing. He forgets where he left his straw hat, forgets where the car's parked, forgets Carol's name sometimes, and mine, when I'm there every other day. He smiles at us like we're just two of the circling colours on his rink. Or in summer, two brown deer come down from the hill to watch him stand still in his yard.

We may never know.

We're not to go near it, no matter how it pulls. On pain of death we're not to go near it, let alone stroke it with the flats of our hands. So many coats, always the same, saving the paint cans in the shed. It's growing. Ever so slowly. Like a skull pushing up through the grass.

THE BACK OF THE BEAR'S MOUTH

GOD KNOWS HOW long Carson was watching me before I caught on — it was dark where he was sitting, like he'd brought some of the night in with him. I matched his look for a second, and a second was all it took. He stood up out of his corner and made for the bar.

I saw this show on the North one time. About the only part I remember was these bighorn sheep all meeting up at the salt-lick. They were so peaceful, side by side with their heads bent low, and no rutting or fighting, no matter if they were old or up-and-coming, no matter if they were male or female, injured or strong. That's the way it was with me and Carson. Neither one of us said much. We just sat there side by side, and it felt like the natural thing.

When the time came, Carson just stood and made for the doorway, the same slow bee-line stride he'd taken to the bar. Beside me, the bartender cleared our glasses and talked low into his beard. 'Think twice little girl, the Northern bushman's a different breed.'

But then Carson looked back at me over his shoulder, and just like a rockslide, I felt myself slip off the barstool and follow.

The truck took its time warming up, so we sat together in the dark, both of us staring at the windshield like we were waiting for some movie to start.

'Robin,' he said finally, 'I figure you got no place to go.'

I turned my head his way a little. I was just eighteen and he must've been forty, but none of that mattered a damn.

'No Carson, I don't.'

'Well.' He handed me a cigarette and put one to his own lips, leaving it hanging there, not lighted. I brought the lighter out of my coat pocket and held the flame up in front of his face, the flicker of it making him seem younger somehow, a little scared.

After a minute I sat back and lit my own.

I must've fallen asleep on the drive. It was no wonder with the hours I'd been keeping — hitching clear across the country in just under three weeks. God knows how I landed in Whitehorse, except I remember hearing some old guy in a truckstop talking about it, calling it the stop before the end of the line.

I opened my eyes just as Carson was laying me out on the bed. The place was dark and cold as a meat locker. It stunk of tobacco and bacon, oiled metal and mould and mouse shit, but somewhere underneath all that was Carson's smell — a gentle, low-lying musk. I know it sounds crazy, but I'll bet that smell was half the reason I went with him in the first place.

I pulled the blanket around me and sat up, watching the shadow that was him pile wood into the stove. He lit the fire, then settled back into the armchair, watching me where I sat. I'd always hated people staring at me. I guess that's why I left school in the end — the teachers and everyone staring at your clothes, your hair, staring into your skull. But Carson was different. His eyes just rested on me, not hunting or digging, just looking because I was there, and more interesting than the rug or the table leg.

Who knows how long we sat like that. I remember him pulling a couple more blankets down from a cupboard, laying one around my shoulders and leaving the other at the foot of the bed.

In the morning sun was all through the place. The bed was an old wrought iron double, with only my side slept in. Coals burnt low in the stove. A grizzly head hung over the bed, mounted with its mouth wide open and the teeth drawn back like a trap.

Carson was nowhere, so I stepped outside and lit a smoke. It was warm, the sun already burning holes in the snow. We were in the bush alright, the clearing was just big enough for the cabin, the outhouse, and the truck. The dirt road that led in to the place closed up dark in the distance, like looking down somebody's throat. A skinny tomcat squeezed out the door of the outhouse and sat washing what was left of one of its ears. The trees grew thick and dark, and the sounds of jays and ravens came falling.

I found Carson round back of the cabin, bent over the carcass of a deer. There was another one in the dust nearby, a buck with small, velvety antlers. Carson looked up at the sound of my footsteps, his eyes all quick and violent.

'Morning,' I said.

'Morning.'

'You get those this morning?'

' — No.'

Something told me to shut up. I walked back round to the door and went inside. The place looked like it hadn't ever been cleaned, so I threw a log in the stove, put the kettle on top, and set about finding some rags and soap.

He never touched me for the whole first week. A couple of times he walked up close behind me and stood there, smelling my hair or something, and I waited for his hand on me, but it didn't come.

The days passed easily. I got the place clean, beat the rugs and blankets, swept out the mouse shit, oiled the table, and washed the two windows with hot water and vinegar. I even stood up on the bed and brushed the dust out of the grizzly's fur. There were gold hairs all through the brown, lit up and dancing where the sunlight lay on its neck.

Carson never thanked me for cleaning up, and I never thanked him for letting me stay. On my eighth night there he turned in the bed and I felt him pressing long and hard into the back of my thigh. He held me tight, but it didn't hurt. He fit into me like something I'd been missing, like something finally come home.

Carson was sometimes gone for part of the night, or all of it. He either went out empty and brought a carcass back, or went out with a carcass or two and came back empty. Usually it was caribou or deer, but one time there was a lynx. He let me touch the fur. It felt just the same as a regular cat — a few hairs came away in my hand.

Time went by like this, me cooking and cleaning and watching, sometimes reading the *Reader's Digest* or some other magazine from a box in the cupboard, sometimes just sitting and smoking on the doorstep, watching the forest fill up with spring. Carson got more comfortable when I'd been there for a while, started teaching me how to shoot the rifle — first at empty bean tins, then at crows and rabbits that came into the clearing. When I finally hit a rabbit, Carson let out a whoop and ran to get it. Then he took the gun from my hands and held the rabbit up in front of my face. Its hindlegs were blown clear off. I felt my fingers go shaky when I reached for its ears, felt tears come up the back of my throat when I took it from him, the soft, dead weight of it in my hand.

One night I got Carson to let me go along. That sounds like I had to talk him into it, but really all I said was, 'Can I come?'

'You can't talk if you do.'

'You heard me talk much?'

' — Alright.'

It was like driving through black paint — the headlights cut a path in front of the truck, and the dark closed up behind us. I had to wonder how Carson found his way around, how he ever managed to get back home. When we got a ways off the main road, he slowed right down and started zigzagging, the headlights swishing over the road and into the bush, then back over the road to the other side.

I was just nodding off when Carson cut the engine, grabbed the gun and jumped out into the dark. I caught a yellow flash of eyes in the bush, then came the shots, the gun blazing once, twice, and the moose staggered into the lights, forelegs buckling, head slamming into the dirt.

Carson pulled a winch out from under the seat and rigged it up to some bolts in the bed of the truck. We got the moose trussed up, but it took us forever to get it in the back.

'This is a big one,' I said, not sure if it was true. I'd only ever seen one from far away, standing stock-still in a muskeg, the way they do.

'Not one,' he said, 'two. Springtime, Robin.'

The next night Carson headed off on his own and I was just as glad. I was still trying to lose the picture of that moose's head hitting the ground.

It seems like it would be creepy being out there in the middle of God-knows-where, Yukon Territory, but I got used to it pretty fast. Even when I was alone it felt safer than any city I'd been through — all those junkies and college kids and cars.

One night though, I woke up slow and foggy, feeling like I couldn't breathe. It took a while for me to realize that tomcat was sitting on me, right on my chest, and when my eyes got used to the dark I could make out the shape of a mouse in its jaws.

I'm no chicken, but that dead mouse in my face scared the shit out of me. I threw the cat clear across the room, and the mouse flew out of its mouth and landed somewhere near the foot of the bed. The tom yowled for a minute, then found the mouse and settled down. I swear I didn't close my eyes until dawn. I just lay there, listening to that cat gnawing and tearing at the mouse, snapping the bones in its teeth.

I'd been out there for a couple of months as close as I could guess, and I had no ideas about leaving. It wasn't that Carson was such great company — half the time he wasn't there, and the other half he was busy skinning something, or cleaning his guns, or doing God knows what round back of the cabin. At night was mostly when we met up. He'd climb into the bed after me, and hold me hard and gentle, always the same way, from the back with me lying on my side. I didn't mind — it felt good, and I figured he was shy about doing it face to face. It made sense, a man who lives out in the bush on his own for so long.

By that time I was sure I was pregnant. I hadn't bled since I'd been there, my tits were sore, and my belly had a warm, hard rise in it. One night when Carson was lying behind me, I took his hand and put it there. I turned my face around to him, and even though it was dark as the Devil, I could tell he was smiling. I don't know that I've felt that good before or since.

I only asked Carson about the hunting once.

'Carson, all these animals — '

The way he looked at me made me think of that first day, when he looked up from that deer like he was a dog and I was some other dog trying to nose in on the kill. His eyes were really pale blue, sometimes almost clear. They didn't usually bug me, but times like that I always thought of that riddle — the man gets stabbed with an icicle, and it melts, and then where's the murder weapon?

It was maybe a week or two later when I woke up to the sound of Carson coming home in the truck. That alone told me there was something wrong — usually he coasted up to the cabin and came in without waking me up. I was lighting the lamp when he threw open the door.

'Can you drive?'

'What's wrong?'

'Can you drive!'

'Yes!'

'Get dressed.'

'What's wrong Carson?'

'Goddammit Robin!'

I crawled out from under the covers and grabbed for my clothes. He jumped up on the bed and stood where my head had been, reaching one hand deep into the grizzly's mouth. I thought he'd lost it for sure, but a second later he jumped back down and stuck a fistful of money in my face, twenties and fifties, a fat wad of them.

'There's more up there,' he said, 'if I don't come back you come and get it, just reach past the teeth and push the panel. And watch you don't cut your hand.'

He shoved the truck keys into the pocket of my red mack.

'Carson,' I said, and my voice came out funny. I was thinking about what he said, about him maybe not coming back.

'Get going. Lay low in Whitehorse. I'll find you.'

'But where will you go?'

'Out in the bush. Get going.'

He touched my hair for a second, then held the door open and pushed me outside.

I got a room at the Fourth Avenue Residence. I didn't check in until morning, after spending the whole night driving around in the dark, scared shitless. When dawn came and I finally saw the road sign I'd been hoping for, I felt about two steps from crazy.

Whitehorse was waking up when I pulled into town. I bought a bottle of peroxide at the Pharmasave, and a big bag of Doritos, then I found the Fourth Ave. And parked around back.

First thing I did in my room was eat that whole bag of Doritos, fast, like I hadn't had anything for days. Then I took the scissors from the kitchen drawer and cut off all my hair. It fell onto the linoleum and curled around my feet, shiny black as a nest of crows. I left the peroxide on until it burned, and when I rinsed it out and looked at myself in the mirror I had to laugh. And then I had to cry.

I slept the whole day and through the night, and the next morning I went down to the front desk and bought a pack of smokes, two Mars Bars and a paper. I folded the paper under my arm and didn't look at the front page until I was back in my room. I ate the Mars Bars while I read, and my hunger made me remember the baby. Our baby — mine and Carson's.

PITLAMPER GOES TOO FAR

Conservation Officer Harvey Jacobs was shot and badly wounded late last night when he surprised a lone man pitlamping on a backroad off the Dempster Highway. The man who fired at Jacobs is believed to be one Ray Carson, who has a cabin in the area. RCMP have issued a warrant for Carson's arrest and ask that anyone with information pertaining to his whereabouts come forward. Jacobs took a single .38 bullet in his right side. He is currently in intensive care …

I lay on my back on the bed, until it felt like the baby was screaming for something to eat. I thought about going out, but I ended up calling for pizza.

I was in the corner store when I heard. The old bitch behind the counter leaned across to me and said, 'Did you hear? They got that nut case, Carson.'

I looked down at the lottery tickets, all neat and shiny under a slab of plexiglas.

'They had to take the dogs in after him. Got him cornered up in the rocks of a waterfall, but he turned a gun on them. Well, they had to shoot him, the stupid bugger —'

She kept on talking, but that was the last I heard. I closed the door on her voice, walked up the road a ways, and sat down in the weeds. I thought about staying there forever, thought about the grass growing up around my shoulders, turning gold and seedy, then black and broken under the snow.

Then I thought about the baby and figured I better get up.

BAPTISTE

Sleep. Oh God, yes — sleep.

His forehead kisses the wheel and he wakes, hands frantic, boot slamming the brake. It's alright. The rig's parked. He remembers now — he's out front of a truckstop, pulled up on the shimmering lot.

It's a slow afternoon, one table and a scattering at the counter. He slips into the smoke and gentle clatter, slides into the booth by the door.

'See that one?' The waitress drops a fistful of creamers into her apron, sitting a coke down in front of her weedy son. He nods, head sunk in a comic. She drags a hand through her hair, plucks out a bobby pin and jabs it back. 'For Chrissakes, Darren. *Look* at him.'

She turns her back, pours four fast coffees and heads for her table of truckers. Two of them broad and gentle-eyed, one wiry and mean, one hunched, hairy and secret. Cows, a coyote and a mole. She takes their orders, smiles at their jokes, the soft tone they take with women who aren't their wives. Her eyes skip to the young man. He's only been in a few times, but she remembers him well — always solo, always quiet, always drops a good tip. He looks like hell. She finds herself walking softly, almost creeping as she nears his table.

'Afternoon,' she says gently. 'What can I get you?'

'Coffee.' Like he's not sure what it means. A motherly pang rears up in her chest.

'Nothing to eat?'

Something sour sifts up from his clothes. He's pasty, socket-eyed, the whites shot through with blood.

'Just coffee.'

She returns and he drinks it black, fast enough to be hurting his throat. She pours again, hesitates, then leaves him with the cup at his lip. His eyelids flicker. His head dips down and he shakes it, crying out for a refill, his voice turning the truckers in their seats.

She pours slowly. 'Looks like you're on a long run.'

'A long run,' he parrots. 'Yes.'

'No sleeper in your rig?'

'I — haven't been using it much.' His hands range over the table, fall on a napkin and twist it.

'Sure you won't have something? A piece of pie?'

'No. Thank you.' He stares into his cup. She turns to go, but he stops her, his fingers springing up to close on her wrist. 'Do you remember your dreams?'

She doesn't pull away. It's the way he's looking up at her, like a baby looks up out of its crib. 'I guess so — some. Why?' No answer. 'Do you?'

'Only one.' His eyes darken, as if the pupils are bleeding black. 'It's night, and there's water as far as I can see. I'm not swimming or anything, I'm above it, kind of — hovering.' He shows her with a floating hand. 'At first it looks like I'm alone, but then I realize there's people, the water's full of people, so many you couldn't hope to count. I can barely make them out — really all I can see is their eyes, like they're lit from inside, like jack-o-lanterns.' His grip tightens. 'The thing is, they start to drown. All of a sudden the water gets rough, you know, swirling, and before I know it, it's sucking them down. I try to grab them — their hands, their hair, anything. I try to dive after them even, but I can't. I can't move. They go down while I watch. While I hang there like a goddamn cloud.' His fingers slacken, fall away from her wrist. 'That's it. That's when I wake up.' He laughs hollowly. 'Funny how you can never really do justice to a dream.' He taps a fingertip to his temple. 'Never make it like it is in here.'

She rubs her cloth over the corner of his table, scrubbing a cigarette scar. 'How come — ' she says finally, 'how come only that one?'

'Simple.' He glances away. 'It comes calling every time I sleep.'

Across the shafting light, the mole crushes a smouldering butt.
'Hey Lorraine. We're starin at empty cups here.'

'Alright.'

She crosses to their booth, feeling the coffee-cramp clear up to
her shoulder. For a second she flashes on the pot dropping, breaking
open like a black flower in their midst.

The coyote shoves his cup at her. 'What's with him?'

She lets a little slop over into his saucer. 'Promise you won't say?'
The four of them lean into her, hungry to hear. 'Says he killed a
man,' she whispers, rocking up on her corns. 'Some nosy trucker.'

She feels the outside air on the backs of her arms, turning in
time to see the door easing shut, the dreamer striding away to his
truck. At his table she finds a five tucked under the ashtray. An extra
big tip, like a goodbye.

Semis idle in the dust, the road winding off into pitch pine wilderness both ways. He pauses at the back of his rig, inhaling their
meadowy breath, the stink of their shit-soaked straw. He presses his
hand flat over a breathing hole, until curiosity draws a calf to the
other side. Its nose on his palm, searching, then its tongue.

In the cab, he grinds knuckles into his eyes. His thoughts splinter
and float free — he feels himself sinking, the dream
winding around him, dragging him down. He reaches blindly for
the radio, twisting the knob up high. *Tumbling Dice.* He shakes free
with seconds to spare, releasing the maxi and jamming the truck
into gear.

Pearson International, crowds whirling like clouds of flies. Maggie
can smell herself. The scotch weeping out her pores, the smoke and

stranger-sex in her hair, her skin. She steadies herself on the ticket counter, holding a handful of cash out to the agent — a close-eyed, immaculate woman. 'The first flight to Edmonton,' she whispers, and the agent starts typing, dragon nails on the keyboard, gazing deep into the screen.

'Return?'

'No. Well — yes.' Maggie hangs her head. 'It doesn't matter.'

'Window or aisle?'

'It doesn't matter.'

The agent smiles thinly. 'No baggage?'

When the plane levels out, Maggie lets go of the armrest, uncramping her fingers to accept coffee in a shallow cup. She sips with eyes half-shut, rewinding to the night before.

She'd had way too much. The warehouse was shaking with music, the crowd closing in on her, bleeding colour and sound. Where was Stephane? She'd lost sight of his white-blond head for what felt like forever. Low laughter, a funhouse hall, tall doorways like teeth in a smile. She chose a blue doorknob and twisted. The girl had no head, a body bent over a chair. Stephane was like moonlight — his hair, his bare ass, his eyes and teeth when he turned — everything perfect and chill. Air. She needed air, and the long iron fire escape felt safe. The dark suit must have followed. He spoke softly, led her down the metal twist to his car. Then nothing. An ocean of blackness, until she washed up on his bed like a starfish, wearing nothing but her chunky high heels.

Climbing into the taxi she thought of the loft — Stephane in their bed and probably not alone. The driver turned in his seat. 'The airport,' she pleaded, 'fast.'

The flight attendant offers chicken or fish, and Maggie tastes vomit in her throat. She scrambles over a sleeping child and lurches down the aisle. The cubicle's bitterly bright. She hangs her face over the bowl, throws up the coffee, the night before — the past several years of her life.

The road unrolls, an endless grey snake with a yellow stripe for danger. He's been afraid to lie down for a week. It did the trick for a while — dozing against the door of the cab, an hour at most — until the dream got wise. It gave up waiting for the darkest hour. Started showing up early for work.

Now he takes minute-naps, holding his arm up so he wakes when it falls. Things are losing shape — road bleeding into trees, trees feeding the sky. He can't seem to summon a human face, even that of the waitress a hundred miles back.

Evergreens. Ravens. Road slithering away.

Maggie punches the number, hangs up fast and stands back from the payphone, staring. After a moment she snatches the receiver and punches again.

'Wolfe's den.' A woman. Maggie can't remember her name — it's probably a different one anyway — it's been over a year since she called.

'Is Bill there?' Her voice comes out reedy, blowing in her throat.

'Who's calling?'

'His daughter.' Maggie can't resist. 'Not to worry.'

'Just a minute.' The sing-song is gone. Maggie twists out a little smile. Her hands tremble, digging for a cigarette, lighting it. He takes his sweet time getting to the phone.

'Daughter!' He sounds like a ringmaster, *la-deees and gentlemen*.

'Hi Dad.'

'To what do I owe this honour?'

She draws a fat lungful of smoke. 'I'm at the airport.'

'My airport?'

'I just got in.'

'Damn.'

'What?'

'No no. Always the sensitive soul. No, it's just that we're literally walking out the door, to the airport actually, how do you like that for a coincidence?' He chuckles. 'Dirty weekend in DR.'

'Oh, oh. Well I — '

'That's the Dominican Republic, if you didn't know.' He talks over top of her, gaining speed. 'You're welcome to the condo. How long are you here for? I'll leave you the key — '

'No. No, I'm just passing through.' She matches him, racing to the end of the call. 'I just thought I'd say hi.'

'We could meet for a quick drink? You'll like Lena, she's in show biz too.'

'Oh no. No. I won't be here for long.'

'Well.' Relief in his voice. 'Cab's waiting.'

'Yeah. Well, bye.'

'Bye-bye, princess.' Dial tone empties into her ear. She slams the phone down hard in its cradle, lifts it and slams it again.

He's sick of the radio, the brutal songs, the lunatic ads in his ears. Instead he sings to himself, mumbling a blue streak of nonsense, beating the dash with the heel of his hand. He can feel the cows huddled behind him. In the driver's side window, the sun drops suddenly, taking cover in the swayback hills.

Maggie sits with her back to the bus station wall. Natives shuffle like spirits, filtering through ashtrays and whispering for change. The PA spits ear-splitting static, kids howl through their Smarties and a fat mother slaps one of them, hard. An hour passes like this, and another, until a monotone garble breaks in. 'GreyGoosefor SaintAlbertNestowTawatinaw andpointsnorthward NOW loadinat BAY FOUR.'

Maggie detours at the bathroom, taking forever to pee, swollen and tender, shameful. She swings the steel door and catches sight of herself in the mirror. Too thin — she understands this instantly — sickly even, hair hanging in rags. She soaps her long fingers. Down the far end of the sinks, an old hooker leans in close to her reflection, painting a thick red smile.

The bus driver's a plain, spreading woman with brown hair fine as a child's. Maggie hands her the ticket, ducks into the gloom and drops into a seat, curling her legs up to claim the place beside. The driver wraps a hand around the lever, but before she can draw the door shut, two overgrown boys crash up the stairs. They moan as they pass Maggie's seat, one of them saying *pussy* out the side of his mouth. She holds her breath. Stares out the window until they're past, collapsed in the triple back seat.

The driver swings and seals the door, backing out and shifting, pulling forward into towering lights.

Downtown falls away. The bus eases into bungalow-lined roads, blacktop and suburban sway.

——

Instinct keeps the truck on course, his hand dangling like a dead bird from the top of the wheel, responding to the highway's brilliant spine. His body's howling for sleep, but the dream's close by — he can feel it, crouched low on the seat beside him. He plays a little game, his eyes darting to the odometer — twenty kilometers more, he tells himself, then I'll pull over.

He blinks a long blink, his eyelids crawling up to find the stripe still there, the road razor-straight to the valley's black floor. A yellow sign warns him, but it's just a bright picture, a toy truck on a fat wedge of cheese. The speedometer mounts, throwing ghostly green light up his arm. His eyes drop shut, the dream nudges him, and he's gone.

The engine rides up to the top of the gear, a whimper to a wail, and hearing it, the cows begin to low. Trees give way to houses, nestled small and motionless into the night. It's near midnight and few are awake — a teenage girl at her window, an old war amp who sleeps like a sentry, starting with every shift in the air. The girl feels her heart mount up and race away with the truck's passing speed. The old soldier knows the sound of a runaway. He salutes the night sky, then picks up the receiver and dials.

The highway narrows into Main Street, the cab dancing red–gold–green as lit-up signs slide by. Two drunks swing at each other in the street. They feel the truck's thunder, leap and roll to lie knotted like lovers at the curb. Inside Buffy's Tavern, the peeler catches sight of it first. She points out the window like doomsday, getting better applause than she has all night. In the Chinaman Trading Co. the old man glances up from his books. The truck fills his window, a silver, illusory wall.

The rig crosses River Road at the foot of Main, jumps the curb, flattens a row of saplings and careens into the dust of the trainyard. One set of tracks, then the second — the cows thrown together, legs buckling, skulls slamming into steel. He comes to on the third bone-rattling bounce of rail, his eyes snapping open to find water, wild and violent, just beyond the glass. The river explodes. He thrusts a boot into the brake and wrenches the wheel, sending the tail of the truck flying, wheels ripping from the rivermuck as the rig slams onto its side. The breath's torn from his chest as he hits the far door and blacks out.

The trailer doors burst. The herd spills into the river, splashing into the black, legs broken, hide bleeding where the bone's cut through.

The Chinaman opens his door on people pouring by. Even Buffy leaves the bar, pausing to rip off her apron, wrestling it over heavy breasts and a halo of frosted hair. The air swells with sirens. Phone lines light up like fuses across town, babies wailing, dogs baying and pacing their yards.

Vehicles wheel into the trainyard — pick-ups, beaters, sedans — they line up along the bank, shining their highbeams on the scene. Two fire trucks throw red light over the crowd, men in uniform shouting, telling everyone to keep back — but it's too late.

People are in the water, up to their waists, their chests, putting them-selves between the cows and the depths, clinging to warm necks and pulling the beasts toward land.

A mountie and two paramedics scale the truck, feeling it shift beneath them, settle deeper into the river's bed. They lift the driver's-side door and crouch like graverobbers, shining torches into the pit of the cab. The paramedics reach down, grab one boot each and pull — God knows if he'll come up in one piece, but there's no other way — water's climbing up the cab, his head and torso already submerged. They work him past the steering wheel and up into the air, laying him out on the trailer's cool side. He's all there — he gags and starts breathing with a little help, vomiting a lungful of river. They lower him on a stretcher, past the truck's muddy belly, the chaos of people and cows. An ocean of eyes, reflecting back head-lights from the river's black pull. He screams. He's still screaming as they feed him to the ambulance and slam the back doors.

The cows know no direction — many wander into the deep before anyone can stop them, the current lifting them like bewil-dered brides. They'll wash up on a deadfall days later, or lie bloated in back-eddy shallows, with raven beaks ripping their hides.

The calves go quickly, their bodies light in the river's arms. The mothers, dragged to shore, plunge back into the water as the heads of their young swirl away. The crowd works on, hauling the cows back to land, tying them to bumpers and tree trunks, staggering into the water again. It's past one in the morning when the river rips the last calf from a young man's hands and bears her away. Almost half the cows and most of the calves are gone. People stand stunned and silent on the bank, the river running out of their clothes. Straining on tethers, the remaining cows bellow and keen.

Elsie Mahoney wheels into the trainyard and makes for the wreck. She piles out of the car, blankets in her arms, her loose white hair collecting light as she limps to the gathering at the river's edge. She distributes the blankets, moving slowly through the murmuring crowd. Cars and trucks keep coming, headlights swinging through the black. Those with children have brought them along. Most are asleep in back seats, but a few play wildly, hurling sticks at the river, happy in the swirling dark.

—

Seven blocks from the river, the bus rolls to a stop outside the Baptiste Burger Bar Drive-in. Maggie can taste onion rings. Summers with her mother and grandmother — she'd bite into a hot, oily ring, grasp the slick onion and draw it out. The women laughing, crows gathering as she flung the limp innards away.

In the dead of night, the drive-in's deserted. A huge plastic burger looms over the roof, lit from within, glowing golden buns across the lot. Maggie steps down from the bus and the door folds shut, the driver pulling her soft hair back in a knot, then easing away, pointing the blunt nose of the bus north. Maggie crosses to the payphone. Thirteen rings before a woman answers, her voice slack with sleep.

'Baptiste Taxi.'

'I need a cab at the Burger Bar.'

'He's down at the crash.'

'Pardon me?'

'He'll be right there, honey.'

—

Elsie stares out over the rushing black, the carcass of the truck lying half-submerged. The river's strong in her nose, rich and rising, the cottonwoods sharp and clean. She flies back through forty-odd years, alighting on a late spring night.

That year the thaw came fast, the river mad through the valley, dirty and wild. She was working late those nights, cramped in the attic office of the Brown Bull Pub. There was plenty to catch up with, after a year with a colicky baby. She'd sleep now, Elsie rocking the swing cradle with her knee while she worked. The accounts lay tangled like great lengths of fishing twine — she took hold of a thread, followed it until it came free, then reached in and took hold of another. She could feel him in the floorboards beneath her feet, loud and dull, the sound of drink.

She heard footsteps on the stairs, pulled open the door before the barmaid had a chance to knock. The girl was uncomfortable, shifting from one long leg to the other — it seemed Mr Mahoney was drunker than usual. He'd left the bar untended, gone down to the river with a gang of men.

She left the girl with the baby, took the steep stairs briskly, out through the smoke and curiosity, into the night. At the foot of the street she could make out the shapes of half a dozen reeling men, their laughter arcing back at her through the dark. Anger came up hard and sudden in her chest. The sight of them, wobbly on their legs like newborn colts. The men giggled nervously as she drew near, whispering like children, parting ranks to let her pass. Beyond, her husband stood with his back to her, his brute arms lifted, the river beating hard about his waist.

'Y'see, ya cowardly bastards,' he bellowed, 'it's not so cold! It's gorgeous!'

When no cheers came, he turned to find her small and fierce before him, her shoes sinking deep in the mud. The men behind her looked down at their boots. She stared at him, stared through his skull as the river gripped him in its icy hands.

'Mick Mahoney,' she spit the words, 'get out of there before you catch your death.' She turned on her heel, the men following like penitents, trailing after her back to the bar.

Mick came last, dragging himself to the bank like a near-drowned dog. The wind ripping into him as he watched her move further away.

Elsie turns her back on the water. Upstream, the crowd begins to break up.

———

The cab comes yellow through the night, the driver leaning across to swing open the door. 'Evening.'

'Hi.' Maggie sinks into the front seat. 'I'm going to the Mahoney place, out on — '

'I know where it is, used to take the old man home a couple times a week. He always tipped real well.' He turns onto the road that reaches out into the country west of town. 'You the grand-daughter?'

' — Yes.'

'You used to come up here with your mother, in the summers.'

Maggie slumps down a little. 'That's right.'

'You're the spitting image, you know that?' He grins. 'I remember when she left town with your daddy. Lotta young men were pretty choked to see her go, especially with some whiz kid from another town.' He pulls a cigarette deck down from his visor. 'I was real sorry to hear about her passing. So young.'

'It was a long time ago.'

Her small hand curled like a bird in the nest of her mother's fingers. The two of them walking the dust road with Freezies hanging from their mouths, the sweet ice staining their lips blue. It's some time before she realizes he's still talking.

'Can you beat that?'

'I'm sorry?'

'How is it he didn't wake up? All the way through town and into the river. Must be drugs.'

'Oh. Yeah.'

'Or suicide. Seems strange though, to do it like that, a load of livestock in the back.'

Down at the crash. She pieces together what he's been saying, realizing she's arrived on the night of a disaster. 'Was the driver — killed?'

'Who knows. Like I said, they hauled him away screaming. Fair few calves lost, though, and some of the mothers.'

She turns her face away, barely aware of her tears until he presses a red handkerchief into her palm.

'I remember when you were little, you know.' He pats the back of her hand. 'You were a sweet kid. Serious, though.'

They ride on in silence, the pale birch waving, and beyond, the glittering slough.

⟨⟩

Blinding light. Hands travel over his body — a woman murmurs low in his ear. Heaven? he thinks. Then pain. The hands press down on his broken ribs and he cries out, realizing he's still alive.

⟨⟩

As the cab draws up to the foot of the drive, Maggie folds the wet handkerchief and hands it back.

'Thanks.'

'I'll take you to the door.'

'No, I'd rather walk. I haven't been here for a long time.' She pays him, includes a generous tip. He waits until she disappears around the first bend in the drive, then pulls away slowly, lights sweeping the brush as he turns back toward town.

It's dark as pitch, three bends to go before the verandah light. Jack pines tower down the drive, swaying black against the star-heavy sky. Something scuttles in the brush. She freezes, heels sinking in the gravel, as the growl of a car engine winds suddenly through the trees.

Elsie spots her at the last moment. The wheels spit stones, spinning to a stop as the figure drops from sight. She thrusts the lever into park, throws open the door and struggles out. In the pool of the headlights, a young woman sits up, lifting a dark curtain of hair with her bloodied hand.

'Maggie, my God — ' Elsie falls to her knees.

'I'm okay, I'm fine.'

'Did I hit you?'

'No, no it's — ' She laughs harshly as Elsie helps her to stand. 'It's these fucking shoes.'

An Irish setter comes bounding to the car, behind her a small woolly shadow, a malamute pup. Elsie pats the setter's flank, stooping to gather the pup in her arms.

'This is Maggie, gang, the prodigal granddaughter.' She takes Maggie's hand, laying it gently on the big dog's back. 'This is Caley. She was thrown from a car out on Munns Road, can you imagine the black-hearted bastard?' She shakes her head. 'I haven't named the little one yet — got him at Jim Coulter's just the other day. He was putting a litter down with a bat when I came to pick up my eggs. This here was the last in line.' She places the puppy in Maggie's arms. 'Seems I'm attracting strays.'

Maggie cries when Elsie touches alcohol-soaked cotton to her scrapes. She climbs into bed, sleeping suddenly, like a play-worn child. Elsie tucks the covers down and backs out of the room. Leaves the door open to let in the light.

It's late morning when the replacement truck arrives. Eighty miles left to the Hogarth ranch. Hogarth himself has driven down to watch over what's left of the herd, bringing two jumpy cattle dogs and a big, silent son. They've smoked and waited since hours before dawn, Hogarth cursing about the crash to those that come and go, the son now and then signalling the dogs to hem in a stray. Most of the cows keep close, browsing the riverbank grass.

Their eyes widen when the new driver lowers his ramp. The men try to guide them up into the dark metal cave, slapping their rumps, setting the dogs barking and nipping their shins. The herd shifts nervously but holds ground. In the end, the men take switches to them, howling like lunatics, driving them in a thundering stampede.

As the rig pulls out of the yard onto River Road, Hogarth enlists a couple of onlookers to help heft a dead cow into his pick-up. It was shot between the eyes the night before, when a mountie found it slumped on broken legs. The men lay it out in the bed, neck bent, hindlegs dangling out the tailgate. Hogarth fastens the carcass down with a length of yellow rope, while his son ties an orange rag around one of the overhang hooves. On the way back to the ranch the dogs ride in the cab, noses pressed to the cow's head, a thin pane between them and the bloody brown eyes.

Hogarth will butcher the body for the deep freeze. No sense letting it go to waste.

When the pick-up's dust settles, people turn from the river and wander back to their lives. The town buzzes with the news of the crash — those who missed it head down to the banks, or pump the witnesses for details, leaning forward in their chairs, closing their eyes to see the truck's long body flip like a rodeo-thrown steer.

Retired farmers talk round-robin in the Nostalgic Cafe.

'Lucky any were saved.'

'More'n half taken.'

'A waste is all, a vicious waste.'

Down the street, Buffy welcomes the first, thirstiest drinkers of the day. All afternoon long she talks of the crash while pulling sudsy mugs of draft, returning again and again to a calf dragged helpless into the deep, the mother following, giving herself up to the pull. Every time she tells it, she pours three fingers of Wild Turkey and knocks it back. By late afternoon, she's pie-eyed and weepy, and drinks are on the house.

The women in Pearl's Unisex Salon cluck their tongues, heads full of the night, ears ringing with splashes and shouts.

'You get a look at that driver?' one of them asks.

'Never mind look, did you hear how he screamed?'

Maggie bows her head until it rests on the kitchen table. Elsie fixes her own tea, just milk, and Maggie's, milk and a big spoonful of honey. Maggie's taken everything black ever since she left home, but she drinks greedily, licking the rim of the cup. She reaches for her cigarettes, but Elsie lays a hand over the pack. 'Outside if you want to smoke.'

'What? You quit?'

'Yep.'

'Chimneystack Mahoney?'

'Changed my spots.'

'Wow.' Maggie plays with the lighter, making the flint spark.

Elsie sips her tea, gazing at Maggie, the blue half-moons under familiar eyes. The last time they sat together at this table, Maggie was stumbling into womanhood. She was tall for her age, willowy and intense, beginning to keep secrets.

Maggie glances out the window, startled by the knee high grass, the weedy chaos of the grounds. 'What happened to the yard?'

'No groundskeeper.'

'Why?' Maggie asks warily. 'Where's Ed?'

'Hospital. Lung cancer.' Simple enough words. She's thought them so many times.

'Jesus, Gran, why didn't you tell me?'

Elsie lifts her eyebrows.

'Oh God.' Maggie dissolves into tears. 'I'm sorry I haven't written, or called. I've been — '

'Never mind, love.' Elsie stands, pressing Maggie's head to her chest. 'You're here now.'

———

They see far fewer runaways than they used to in Baptiste, ever since the advent of air brakes that lock on when the system loses pressure. Even if he had lost his brakes somehow, why hadn't he taken a runaway lane? Asleep at the wheel, of course. But asleep all that way? All the way through town? People start to wonder about the man who drove into the river. The cattle-crash man.

A nurse's aid gets a break and hurries down to the Nostalgic to field questions. She orders her usual, then fusses in her purse, letting the tension build. 'They've got him on tranqs,' she announces finally. 'He's sleeping like a babe.'

The old men at the counter mutter and preen. The bus girl sits a coffee down on the aid's table, her wiping cloth hidden behind her back. 'Wha'd he say?'

'Not much yet.' The aid empties three creams and a stream of sugar into her cup. 'Mostly a lot of raving.'

'Raving?' One of the regulars swings round on his stool. 'About the crash?'

She hesitates, having heard everything second hand. 'He's in shock,' she says finally. 'People say funny things when they're in shock.'

Niko glances up from the paper he has spread over the cash. 'Crazy?'

'Too early to say.'

'Drunk?'

'Nothing in his blood. Not even trucker speed.' She answers quickly, beginning to feel uneasy, like she might be saying too much. Her hot turkey arrives and she tucks in, thankful for the excuse to shut up.

Strays turn up throughout the day, stunned, lowing wanderers dropping pies. One drinks from the City Hall fountain. One's found bleeding out back of the Baptist Church.

Word spreads through town that the cattle-crash man has two cracked ribs and a couple of cuts. Nothing serious, but they're holding him for observation. In other words, he might be nuts.

Anyone can go crazy. Remember the long winter when Tom Simchuk lost his wife to pneumonia? He chased two kids on skidoos through town in his rusty Ford — him waving his twelve gauge out the window, the boys breaking away through the lumber yard, bullets splitting the air beside their ears. Tom got off with a warning, told the mounties they cut him off, nearly put him tits-up in the ditch. Everyone got used to his jumpy eye — the slow, spooky dance of his voice.

People feel for the cattle-crash man.

'He'll be out of a job now. Never drive truck again, that's certain.'

'He got any family?'

'You see anybody showing up?'

The aid returns to the Nostalgic with the latest. 'He's awake,' she tells them. 'Gentle as a kitten and quiet as the grave.'

He looks away when they ask how it happened, shakes his head when they want to know who they should call.

⸺

Elsie perches on Ed's bed, pressing his hand like a charm between her palms. She watches the nurse hold a needle to the light, snap the nail of her index finger against it three times, smile brightly and slide the tip into the mouth of the IV. Relief shines in his eyes. His words break apart, he sinks into a mutter, as though the pain was all that kept him making sense.

She lays down his hand. Thumb like a fishhook, skin papery, blood winding through slow blue veins. She feels the ghost of his palm, hard as shoe leather on the soft underside of her breast.

A moan from the next bed brings her back. She stands and smoothes her skirt, the arthritis like a weasel, hanging by its teeth at her hip. She bends to kiss Ed's cracked lips, then turns and hobbles out of the room.

She stops in the lobby, piling two overstuffed shopping bags on the desk. The nurse looks up from her nail file, smiling. 'More stuff for the auxiliary shop?' She fingers the fine, bright wool baby clothes.

'You make the best stuff they got in there, you know that?'

'You're damn right.' Elsie reties a small bow at the neck of a jumper. 'Some excitement last night.'

'I'll say.'

'That driver still here?'

'I don't know if *here*'s the right word.'

'Where've they got him?'

The nurse brings up his record on her screen. 'Ward A. One-seventeen. Hasn't made a peep so far.'

Elsie sees the cows, tied back from the river, bellowing in the dark. 'Think I'll get a coffee.' She skirts the stale odour of the cafeteria, following the signs to Ward A.

At room 117 she looks both ways like a thief, closes her hand on the doorknob and ducks inside. It's dim, mustard curtains drawn closed on the sun. He sits propped in white pillows, wide eyes watching as she approaches the foot of his bed.

'Hello son.'

He says nothing. She lifts the clipboard and slips her glasses from the pocket of her skirt. 'Sean Bogue — now there's a fine Irish name. I'm a Mahoney, a Hughes before that. You born over there?' Silence. She leans gently on the edge of his bed. 'If you're not feeling talkative, that's fine. You want to be alone, you just touch my hand and I'll go.' He doesn't move. 'I wanted to tell you something.' She pauses. 'I just about drove into that river too. Not the same spot, mind you, a little further upstream.'

He touches her little finger. She stands to go, but his hand folds over hers, holding her fast.

'You look tired, son.'

He nods. Her hand locked in his, she eases him down, pulling the sheet up around his chest. A tune rises in her head. Slowly, softly, she begins to sing. 'Over in Killarney, many years ago — '

He closes his eyes.

'Me mother sang a song for me in tones so sweet and low — '

A few more lines and his breath deepens and drags. She sings the lullabye through, then works free of his hand, laying it down with infinite care.

—

Elsie drives through morning light, the old red swimsuit slack under her dress. She never takes underwear for the ride back, enjoying the feel of the out-of-doors. Imagine an accident, a sixty-nine year old woman caught driving with no panties. No doubt they'd credit senility.

She noses the Dodge into its customary spot, the dogs leaping from the back to disappear down the rocky trail. Elsie takes her time, walking carefully, watching for trip roots as she goes.

The dogs range the shallows as she wades into the lake. Water swallows her thighs, she shuts her eyes and dives, doing the breast-stroke like kids do, dunking her head. She couldn't believe her eyes the one and only time she tried the Lion's pool — made-up women swimming stiff, timid laps, emerging with bone-dry hair.

She pulls toward Black Rock, the small barren island in the center of the lake.

Baptiste Lake. These are the waters she learned to swim in, her father crooking his arm under her belly, telling her to kick like the Devil.

She rolls over to float on her back. Dragonflies pair up and fly mating. Blackbirds ride the high cattails, heave their red shoulders and cry.

—

The sun breaks into Maggie's room, shoving fingers of light through the blinds. She burrows down until the glare swings round to the afternoon side of the house, then crawls out and sits cradling her head in her hands. She eats a little, then naps on the verandah until nightfall. Sometimes she walks, following the lie of the land.

Elsie watches her granddaughter wander in a young woman's body. After a few days, she walks into Maggie's room, yanks up the blinds and waits. Eventually, Maggie rolls over. 'What is it?'

'I told Ed you're here. He's asking to see you.'

Maggie lays an arm over her face. 'I'll go soon. Not now.'

'He's at his best in the mornings.'

'No Gran.'

Elsie moves closer, her face sharpening as she leaves the back-light behind. 'Maggie, get out of bed.' That tone, rare but unmistak-able, like biting down on a piece of glass. Maggie hauls herself up.

'Attagirl.' Elsie grins. 'I'll be waiting in the car.'

'Look who's here.' Ed smiles weakly, surfacing from sleep. 'You got big.'

Maggie sways on her feet. 'Hi Ed.'

'And I got small, eh?'

Elsie's pats Ed's shoulder. 'I'll leave you to it for a bit.' She slips away before Maggie can protest, hurrying down the hall to Ward A.

At the click of the door, Sean looks round from the window. Sun floods the room, rising in the hollows of his face. 'Hi.' His voice startles her.

'You're talking.'

'Now and then.'

She draws a stool up beside him. The two of them gaze out the window, a green slope, a scurrying woman in white.

'My mother used to sing that song, the one you sang.'

'Ah, we're a sentimental lot. You can take the Irish out of Ireland but you can't take the Ireland out of us. Listen to me, born and bred in Baptiste.'

'Have you been there?'

'I wanted to go. I'd heard so many stories, my father, and my husband — I had all the books, photos too, magazine clippings. My husband wasn't having any part of it. *Back to that rain-sodden peatbog?* he'd say. *Back to the forty fuckin' shades of green?* ' She sighs. 'Just wasn't meant to be, I suppose. By the time I was free of him, I'd somehow lost the urge.'

'I went.'

'You did?'

'The year I turned nineteen. My old man's uncle in Connemara died and left me a couple thousand pounds. As soon as I found out, I felt like I had to go there, see where he'd lived, his fishing boats, the house where he died.' His face darkens. 'The old man went nuts. He forbade me — I was supposed to be starting at Royal Roads in a few weeks. That's what made up my mind in the end, I guess, him forbidding me.'

'So you went.'

'Yeah. The second that plane left the ground I knew it was over.'

'What was?'

'My life. Cadets, military college, him making me into his little GI Joe. Guns made my gut hurt. Seriously, not even firing them, just picking them up.'

Elsie draws a crude flower in the fine dust on the sill. 'So, what did you want?'

'You think I knew? I still don't.' He stands, holding his thin robe closed. 'I spent most of that winter in my great-uncle's stone cottage, listening to the wind and the rain. I guess I was hoping for a sign. I sat in the pub and listened, I sat by the sea and looked — until spring came and the attorney showed up with a buyer. When I got back home I was broke. No clue what I was going to do. I stayed with my parents for a few days, until things got — out of hand. I worked on a seiner for a year, then a pulp mill, half a dozen other jobs before I started driving truck.'

'You see your folks?'

' — I call my mother sometimes.'

'Hm.' Elsie glances at her watch. 'The bell tolls. I'll come and see you tomorrow.'

He turns to watch her go. 'Mrs Mahoney?'

'Elsie.'

'Elsie. You know what you said about — '

She holds up her hand. 'Another time, sonny. It's a long story.'

Caley twitches in her sleep, a black ant beating a path through the slippery fur behind her ear. Maggie lies limp in the faded hammock, remembering the day Ed drove spikes into these pines and hung the bright cloth — stood back laughing when she jumped in and asked for a push.

Now he's dying. Drying up, like the spider-sucked husk of a fly. It was the same with her mother, the tumour swelling in her womb, a greedy baby, suckling from the inside out.

She stood wedged between her father and Elsie, Grandad Mick off pacing through the weeping trees. She hated the priest — his soft Latin winding, his fluttering hands. She hated her father's heaving shoulders, hated the tears on Elsie's neck, running like a faucet, pooling in the collarbone hollows. She felt as though she could set fire to something with her fingers, maybe the priest's robe, or the black box that lay heavy before him. Her face was white. She swayed over the grave, sweating in her velveteen dress. Elsie felt her forehead and took her home, while men in rolled shirtsleeves lowered her mother away.

Her temperature mounted into the night, Elsie at the bedside with a cloth, the men downstairs, heads hung over an emptying bottle. The fever broke just before dawn. Her father woke soon after and left for the office. Mick rose next and shuffled out to warm up the car. Took the highway north out of Edmonton as fast as his Buick would go, leaving Elsie to stay on until Bill told her she should go home — they'd be fine.

Silence fell over the house. It was as though Katherine had acted as translator between husband and daughter, so skillful she'd convinced them they spoke the same language. They began to talk in fragments, feelings never fitting the words they chose. As time went by, they communicated less and less. They'd pass each other in the hallway, smiling automatically. *How was work? Fine. What did you learn today? Nothing.*

The hammock rocks gently, wind's breath and the hum of flies. Maggie slips like a swimmer into sleep.

She's alone, dressed in red at the mouth of a grave. She lowers herself into the pit, slides her fingers under the coffin's bevelled lid. A body wound in white. She searches for the loose end of the sheet, feeling the corpse give gently beneath her hands. A clod of earth hits her back. She looks up — a ring of blurred faces, like animals bent drinking at a hole. They hold out their fists, drop handfuls of dirt in her eyes.

Sunlight. She struggles from the hammock's net and stands shaking, the dream draining out of her into the grass. The setter sits up to watch her stumble into the woods, then curls a tight circle back to sleep.

Maggie winds deep into the evergreen gloom, through tamarack and fir, birch flickering white in the afternoon slant of the sun. She touches a trunk, the skin of a child, smooth, with small scratches and scars.

The clearing's just as she remembered, thick with white clover and bluebells, Indian paintbrush like smudges of blood. She's never brought anyone here, never even spoken of this place. The old choke cherry stands like a solitary bride, a tent of pale blossoms, humming with honeybee wings. She drops to her knees, crawls to its red trunk and holds on.

———

Sean stands with his nose to the glass.

'How's the patient?' Elsie lets the door fall closed.

'Better.' He turns and leans back against the sill. 'They'll be kicking me out soon, now they know I'm not cracked.'

Elsie laughs. 'What'll you do?'

'Don't suppose I'll be driving.'

'What do you want, Sean?'

He twists away. 'I told you, I don't know.'

'Bullshit. What do you want?'

He leans into the window, his gaze taking him out across the grounds, away. 'Something solid, I guess. Something — alive.'

'Ah ha.' Elsie reaches into her straw bag, draws out a small piece of paper, folds it and presses it into his hand. 'I need a new groundskeeper.' She pauses at the door. 'That's a fancy word for a handyman gardener. You let me know.'

She's gone as suddenly as she came. The hospital grounds stretch into trees, a town, the muscular curves of a river. He opens his fist on her name, her number in dancing green ink.

———

Elsie's had a monthly trim at Pearl's for most of her life, Maggie and her mother coming along in the summers — three faces in the mirrors, like pictures of the same woman, portraits taken over time.

'Pearl, you remember Maggie.' Elsie settles into her chair, pulling the pins from her hair, letting it slip in a white stream down her back.

'I sure do. You look terrific, honey. A little skinny.' She pumps Elsie's chair. 'Aren't you an actress now?'

'Yeah. I'm — taking a break.'

Pearl straightens the pink tunic over her thick waist. 'I don't wonder. What girls go through in your business. Throwing up 'til their teeth rot, getting the ribs cut out of their sides — '

'Pearl — ' Elsie begins.

'No Gran,' says Maggie, 'she's right.'

'You're damn right I'm right.' Pearl turns her attention to Elsie's hair, holding the ends up to the light. 'Maybe not polite, but right.'

Maggie reaches for a *Macleans,* one ear riding their easy talk. She flicks the glossy pages, until a face leaps out at her and she freezes. *LeDuc redefines theatre. Toronto's hot new director may be an enfant terrible* — she lets the magazine fall shut.

The stage was cavernous and bare, lights dangling like blackened seed pods, windows sealed in the stinking heat. She'd been waiting for over an hour, one young, sweating female in a pack of perhaps twenty.

A click sounded in the stage door. They were like dogs at the pound, drawing themselves up to full height, running tongue-tips over lips, leaning forward to shake out their hair. A woman appeared, french twist, tight lips and a loose-fitting suit. Then two small, dark men — possibly twins — one with a clipboard, the other with a camera at his chest. The director came last, casting silence over the crowd. He moved like the wind in wild grass, circling the nearest body, speaking sideways to the woman with pinched lips. 'Too chunky.' The girl's face fell as he turned away. The next had legs too short, another had sad cheekbones, a third was too much like a bird. Breasts too heavy, buttocks too flat, this one too haughty, that one too sweet. By the time the troup halted in front of Maggie, her bowels were a bucket of snakes.

He swayed up against her, reached in under her hair to run a finger down the bones in her neck.

'Whore,' he said quietly.

'What?'

'Whore. You're an actor aren't you? Give me your whore.'

There was no time to think. The word bloomed inside her, she lifted her eyes and breathed perfume out her half-open mouth.

'Her.' He dropped the sound like a glove. The assistant director made small noises in her throat. The camera flashed, and when Maggie could see again, he was gone.

Stephane all but ignored her when she wasn't on stage — it was she who watched him, his liquid height, the eerie light of his hair. A month into rehearsals he caught her off guard, appearing in her dressing room like a dream. She held her hands over bare breasts and he smiled, derision she mistook for delight.

'Maggie.' Elsie's voice. 'Maggie, are you alright?'

'Huh? Oh, yeah.'

'C'mon girly.' Pearl looms over her. 'Time to get gorgeous.'

⊷

Sean counts ten rings. Elsie answers just as he's pulling the receiver from his ear.

'I've been reading gardening magazines.'

'Hurrah. I'll pick you up.'

'Okay. They tell me I can leave anytime.'

'Round noon alright?'

'I'll be waiting.'

He's ready an hour early. Pacing the tiny room, then perching on the bed. Fingering his knitting ribs.

Elsie leads him past the house, across the sloping side field to the groundskeeper's cottage. She follows the ghost of an overgrown path. Ed striding up to the house, his silver hair wet from the shower. The two of them hurrying back hand in hand, the grass wearing away under their new-found youth.

She unlocks the door. 'Lord,' she sniffs, 'it's like a root cellar in here.' She shoves the burlap curtains back and throws open the windows. 'You'll want to get the screens in soon.'

Sean hesitates on the stoop, his eyes wandering — white walls and wood, a dresser, a bookshelf, a rough table and two rail-backed chairs. A small corner kitchen, then a door, then the bulk of a tarnished brass bed.

'The door goes through to the toilet and shower, then back onto the shed.' Elsie turns to him. 'Well, come in for God's sake. This is your place now.'

He clears his throat. 'I'm not sure why you're doing this.'

'I told you, I need a groundskeeper.'

'I know, but why me? I've never really gardened.'

'About time you learned.' She eases past him in the doorway. 'Come on up to the house when you feel settled, we'll have a bite and I'll show you around.'

He watches her limp away through the high grass, then steps

inside and closes the door. Spirits of tobacco and woodsmoke. Then something else, animal yet familiar, a hint of bodies in the dark.

Outside the house, a coil of brown crosses his path. The blood beats hard in his neck as he stoops to watch the snake wind away. A rhythmic, disappearing twist. Above him on the verandah, Elsie sways on a wicker swing.

'Come on in.' She stands and massages her hip. 'I've got lunch ready inside. Come and make yourself useful.'

Sean follows her through the flapping screen door, past a portrait flashing dark in the hall. Elsie with her hair still black, and a hatchet-faced man behind. A young couple before them, arms folded around a slender girl.

Elsie drops a handful of mint leaves into a tall pitcher of tea, arranging glasses and jam cookies on her tray. She gestures to Sean to bring a plate piled high with sandwiches. On the way out, he pauses at the portrait again. The girl watches him. The rest of them pose blindly, but she somehow sees out — staring until he tears himself away.

Elsie pours glasses of tea as he attacks his food. 'Slow down there, you'll swallow your tongue.'

'Sorry, hospital food.'

She eases back into the swing. 'That's the family you saw in there. Me and my husband Mick, my daughter Katherine and her Bill, my granddaughter, Maggie.

'Beautiful family. Is your husband — '

'Dead? Yep.' The ice cracks in her glass. 'He and my daughter, both dead.'

Sean swallows. 'Jesus. I'm — '

'Don't be. It's been years.' She smiles with her eyes. 'Maggie's visiting from Toronto. She's in town at the moment. I'll show you the truck when she gets back.'

Flowerbeds lie choking under last year's dead. He follows Elsie over the land, the dogs loping ahead, scouting and circling back. They ease through an opening in the caraganas, stepping out into crabapple rows. Sucker branches shoot skyward, sapping the trees of their strength.

'Down that way there's plots for corn.' Elsie points toward the tree line. 'It's a bit late for seeding, but I bet we can still squeeze out a crop. We've always grown plenty of corn.' They follow the arc of the hedge past a small, sedgey pond. A hammock sways gently, strung between two tall pines.

'Are the woods all yours?'

'For a mile or so in any direction.' Elsie sweeps her arm like a wing. 'My father always said it was good to have some wilderness around. Mind you, land was dirt cheap when he bought this place.'

She leads him past a wild rosebush, down the stone path alongside the house, past a freshly broken hole. 'Looks like that puppy's a digger.' She kicks at the dirt. 'I've gotten a start in the vegetable beds, there. Whatever you want to know, there's a veritable library in that cottage. Every green thumb do-it-yourself ever written.'

They emerge at one end of the verandah. Beside Elsie's Dart sits an aging Ford half-ton, paint faded to cream of tomato. The engine clicks quietly. No driver to be seen.

⌒

Elsie sits propped among pillows in her bed, a reading lamp trained on the wool in her lap. She slips the yarn over her finger, dips the hook into the last row of a tiny, bright blue jacket. The house sighs around her. Sleep teases, hovering, then lifting away.

⌒

Sean ranges the grounds with an armful of Ed's dog-eared books, touching petals and stamens, clusters and catkins and buds. So much he never knew. Twigs sweat, leaves have teeth, bark bleeds and grows furrowed with age. He squats down by a red wood lily, stares deep into its spotted heart.

——

The Boutique Unique on Main. Maggie piles clothing on the counter, returning to the rack for the dress she tried on without knowing why. The saleswoman has raven hair, falling down her front in two long, beaded braids. She folds everything slowly, keen eyes looking Maggie up and down.

'You the Mahoney girl?'

'Yes. Well, Wolfe, really. My father's Wolfe.'

'Sure, I know Elsie from the bingo.' She arranges Maggie's purchases in two pink plastic bags. 'Staying long?'

'I — don't know really.' Maggie frowns. 'I just kind of landed here. I'm in between — things.'

The woman drums her fingers on the counter. 'Wolfe, huh? How's that cattle-crash man?'

'I'm sorry?'

'Your new gardener. That one who was driving the truck.'

'Oh. He's fine. Doing fine. Thank you.' The door jingles in Maggie's hand.

'Don't forget your stuff.' She holds out the bags with a cryptic smile.

Elsie folds the *Baptiste Herald* and looks over her glasses, bringing the Dart and Maggie into focus. 'Find anything?'

'The basics. I won't have to raid your drawers anymore.'

'Raid my drawers?' Elsie snorts. 'The cheek.'

'Dirty old woman.' She bends to kiss Elsie's forehead. 'I bought a white dress. God knows why — I haven't worn one since my first communion.'

'I remember. My wedding cake on legs.'

'And those tights, all hot and droopy — they were torture.'

'Scarred for life, eh?'

'Yeah, I'll need therapy.' Maggie drops down to scratch Caley behind the ears. 'Gran?'

'Hm?'

'How come you never told me about the new groundskeeper?'

Elsie smiles coyly. 'Told you what?'

'I dunno. Maybe the part about him crashing his rig into the river.'

'Oh, that.' Elsie draws the paper back up in front of her face. 'Must've slipped my mind.'

—

'You the cattle-crash man?' The stock boy speaks sideways, his eyes and hands on the row of seed packets before him.

Sean returns an envelope of pole beans to its hook. 'I guess I am.'

'You're working for Mrs Mahoney now, huh?'

'That's right.'

'That's a way better job than driving truck.' He clears a space on the shelf. 'I'd rather be a gardener any day.'

'Yeah, I like it.' Sean hesitates. 'Is that what they call me around here — the cattle-crash man?'

'I guess.' The boy takes up his price gun, fiddling with the dials. 'We don't know your name.'

'It's Sean. Sean Bogue.'

The boy flashes a shy grin, rips the lid off a carton and starts hammering down a row.

Outside, Sean backs the pick-up into the loading yard, piles sack after sack of steer manure onto the bed. Elsie crosses the lot, loaded down with bags of wool. She climbs into the passenger seat as he's hoisting the last sack onto his shoulder.

'Take a right at the firehall. I'll show you a bit of the town.'

She directs him through quiet streets, past river-muddy children, women steering pale carriages, men tarring a new patch of road. At a stoplight, he wheels left onto Main.

'This is as close as you get to a downtown.'

'It's great. A little like going back in time, but great.'

'The Nostalgic's a good little place, there. This thing's strangling me.' She yanks at her seatbelt. 'Feel familiar at all?'

'Huh?'

'This is the road you came in on.'

The knuckles pull up white out of his hands. 'Oh.'

'Amazing luck, really.'

'Hardly.'

'The way you didn't hit anything? Or anyone, for that matter. The fact that you're still with us — I'd call that lucky.'

'I guess.' He shifts down, feeling suddenly fast and frail. 'I feel bad though, all those cows.'

'I know, they're beautiful creatures, cows.' She pats his knee. 'You see that bar? Buffy's?'

Sean nods without really looking, unwilling to take his eyes from the road.

'It was built by Seamus Hughes, a.k.a. my father. Used to be called the Brown Bull. So much of my life happened in there, and now it's all brass and mirrors, and girls twirling tassels on their tits.' She laughs. 'Take this right, just follow along the river for a while, this is what you might call the scenic route.'

He relaxes a little as the road flattens and opens out. 'Tell me about Seamus.'

'Ah, Seamus. He came over without a penny, made his money running whiskey down south. That was before he clapped eyes on my mother and got a sudden urge to settle down. He bought the property outright and built the house the way she wanted. They had plans alright — they were going to fill that place with children, the Hughes clan spilling out into the countryside. Only my mother was such a little thing. She kept to her bed for just about the whole term with me, and bled til she died when I was born.' She sighs. 'So, in the end it was just the two of us rattling around in that big old barn. He never did get up the steam to remarry. He was too busy with the bar by then anyway.'

'What was it like?'

'Hm?'

'The Brown Bull.'

'Oh, bit of a dump, really. Seamus would never hear of me trying to smarten it up — he said people liked it well enough, and I should learn to leave well enough alone. I suppose he was right. I was never so glad as the day I sold that place. I believe I skipped a little, coming out of there after signing the papers.' She digs in her wool bag, half-burying her face. 'I met my husband there, you know.'

'Mick? Was he a regular?'

'Christ no, I wouldn't touch that lot with a fishing pole.' She laughs. 'Mick was — well, he was different. I was down from the office for a glass of tea one night, when a stranger came walking through the door. Heads turned — I'm not kidding — he was handsome then, a great shock of auburn hair, tall and wiry — you could tell by the look of him he was a drifter. His eyes locked into mine, just like in the movies. He walked straight up and asked me for a whiskey, but Seamus heard his accent and came away from the boys at the end of the bar. He brought down his best bottle of Paddy. *Well now*. I'd never heard his brogue so strong. *It's not often I hear the music of an Irish tone around here. What's your name son?* he asks, and he hands over three fingers of whiskey. The stranger nods, knocks it back in one and says, *Mahoney. Mick Mahoney*. Just like that, emphasis on the *Ma*, let the *honey* die away. Seamus grins and speaks up for the crowd. *Mahoney?* He says it differently, see, emphasis on *hone. Any of you lot know what ma-hone might mean in Irish?* Mick's face goes black and all the men sit forward in their seats. *Anyone?* says Seamus. *Right, ya lot of ignoramuses, it means yer arse — the part we all sit on at the end of a hard day's work!* I could have died, or strangled him with my own bare hands, but Mick just stood there. He waited for the laughter to die down, and for the silence to build up, and then he said, *If you know that much, you'll be sure to know pogue ma-hone.* That was about when Seamus quit grinning. *Ah, you're after forgetting,* says Mick. *It's kiss me arse, grandad. That's it, alright. Kiss me arse.*' Elsie lets out a whoop of laughter.

'Jesus, what happened?'

'Dad poured a double into Mick's glass, poured one for himself and said, *On the house, me lad.* Elsie puffs out her chest, holding up an imaginary glass and pitching her brogue like a leprechaun on TV. *It's the least I can do for a fellow son of Eire.* It wasn't two weeks before Mick was behind the bar, working away alongside the old man. Not much longer before he and yours truly were engaged.'

The lilacs have gone wild on the south-facing wall. Sean kneels in the dirt, nearly faint with their smell, tearing tendrils of morning glory from slender grey trunks. He hears movement through the grass, glances up through the blooms to see a flash of bare arm, a shifting of dark loose hair. The air thickens and catches in his throat.

'Hello?' A hint of fear in her voice.

He's suddenly embarrassed, caught staring at her from behind a bush. He crawls out and stands, eyes circling her uneasy smile. When he speaks, it's with the ghost of a stammer he hasn't heard in years.

'I'm the g-groundskeeper.'

'I'm Maggie.' She slides the cigarettes back into her pocket and holds out her hand.

'Oh. I'm Sean.' He reaches out, then falters, realizing his hand's filthy. She takes it before he can pull back, her handshake a little too firm.

'I'm glad you're saving them. The lilacs.' He shifts on his feet. She breaks from him, taking a quick step back. 'Well. Nice to meet you finally.'

He nods dumbly and she's gone, nearly running she rounds the corner of the house.

He lies alone on top of the sheets, her red mouth returning, her lowered eyes and sideways-settling hair. The ribs ache in his side, hurt him more than they have for days.

Maggie slams the Dart's trunk and jumps into the driver's seat, her blood racing like a child's. Elsie's arthritis is mild — she near skips down the verandah stairs.

At Keening Lake, a quarter mile's wade brings water to the waist, though here and there a sandbar drifts into the air, or a trapdoor drops away in the sand. Wild blueberries reach deep into the shore, driftwood silvers like hair, and horseflies ride bulbous on the breeze. As a girl, Maggie let one or two land before ducking down, watched them slip and float helpless, wings beating the water's skin. It was a science. If you waited too long they took parcels of flesh, leaving evil red welts in their wake.

They shout songs the whole way there, words spilling out the windows into a whirl of dust. At the lake, they set up camp under a row of poplars. Elsie spreads a blue and white blanket over the sand, shapes her towel into a pillow and lies down. Maggie wanders to the edge and wades in.

A legend lies under the lake — the ongoing shallows with their hollows and hills. A heavy wooden sign tells how a little girl drowned in the blink of her mother's eye. The woman searched and cried out for days, until the echo became more than she could bear. Every summer, Maggie stood on tiptoes to read the sign, seeing her own mother, slogging through the water, screaming her name while she played quietly on the floor of the lake.

She mounts a sandbar and stares out over the gentling waves. The breeze brings lilac, a momentary unfurling of scent. In an instant, she's full of his hands — the first part of him she saw — ripping weeds from the necks of trees.

Maggie plunges her hands into hot water as the Dart pulls up outside. The kitchen door swings and Elsie appears, her face pale and drawn. 'Hey now, it's my turn to do those.'

Maggie smiles, running the soapy cloth around the globe of a wine glass. Elsie wanders to the stove to check the bread dough she left rising.

'How is he?' Maggie asks.

'The same. A bit weaker, maybe. I can't seem to judge anymore.' She shakes flour over the counter and eases the dough out of its bowl, her fingers working over the sticky mass.

'Gran, what is Ed to you?'

Elsie draws a deep breath, the heels of her hands resting against the dough. 'A great deal.'

'You love him.'

'Yes.'

'You were lovers.'

Elsie begins rocking against the counter, kneading with her whole body. 'For Christ's sake Maggie, don't say *were* yet.'

Maggie wipes her hands hastily and crosses the room, pressing her face into the silver twist of Elsie's hair. 'You're right, you *are* lovers. I'm sorry.'

Elsie wipes the back of one wrist under her eyes. 'It's alright.' She shifts the stiffening dough a quarter turn, folding it back on itself.

Maggie drifts back to the sink as Elsie divides the dough, forming it into round loaves, two per sheet. She draws a knife across each loaf three times and brushes the scars with oil, then opens the oven and bends into the heat.

'How long,' Maggie begins, 'I mean, when did you — '

Elsie shuts the oven door gently. 'You know how Mick died.'

'Yes. You've never told me, though.'

'It was simple, really — he just took longer than usual fetching the mail. I didn't think anything of it. Sometimes he stopped to fiddle with something in the garage, or else ran into Ed and got talking. I was finishing my tea when I heard something out front, someone pounding up the steps like mad. I knew then, clear as anything, I knew he was dead. I met Ed at the door. *It's Mick*, he said, *call the doctor*, and he ran away down the steps. I suppose I must've called, but I don't remember doing it. I just remember running down the drive, one bend after another, like it would never end. Mick looked older than I'd ever seen him, stretched out flat on the gravel, with Ed bent over him, giving him the breath of life. He pulled me down beside him, took my hands and showed me how to do CPR. Then he put his mouth back over Mick's and we stayed like that, him breathing and me pumping, until the doctor finally came. It wasn't much use — he was dead as a stone. It came as a shock, really. Even with all his drinking, he still seemed strong as a horse. The worst part was we'd been getting along better than we had in years — both too worn out to fight anymore, I suppose.' She shakes her head. 'When we got home from the hospital, Ed made a pot of tea and listened to me talk. I don't know what all I said, but I must've gone on for a couple of hours straight. He just kept filling my cup, boiling the kettle and making more tea. When the women started showing up he went back to the cottage. Says he sat mooning in there for days, afraid to come near and see my grief. Funny how you think you know someone. Ed'd been with us for at least ten years, and I'd never suspected a thing. He waited for nearly a year. The day I left the black in the closet and put on a yellow dress, he came to the door with an armful of daisies.'

In the verandah shade, Elsie hums softly, her hook leading wool through the maze of a cardigan sleeve. Maggie pulls her hair to one side, weaves it into a loose braid, works it apart and begins again. She dozes, waking to find Elsie holding out a fresh loaf, swaddled in a red kitchen towel.

'Take this down to the cottage, will you Maggie? I've made far too much.'

Sean parts the caraganas at the far end of the field, just in time to watch Maggie tie a knot in something red and hang it on the handle of his door. He almost cries out to her, then sees himself — how strange and frantic he would seem. She turns and he counts twenty before setting out across the grass.

The tea towel dropping bright at his feet. Its weight in his hands. Its fragrant weight.

———

Maggie pushes her cutlery to the end of the booth and leans across the table. 'Gran?'

The waitress appears, producing a short pencil from between her breasts. 'Hi Else. The usual?'

'Yep. And one for my granddaughter too. And a couple of vanilla shakes.'

'Oh no — ' Maggie starts.

'A skinny thing like you?' The waitress grins. 'Why the hell not?'

'Okay.'

'Twist your arm, eh?' She hustles back behind the counter.

'Gran?'

'Hm?'

'Were you happy — I mean, were you fulfilled with Grandad?'

'That's some question.' Elsie digs a napkin out of the dispenser. 'I guess I'd have to say no.'

'No? Never?'

'Maybe in the beginning. I don't know that I'd call it fulfilled, though, fascinated is more like it.' She smiles. 'He was wild in those days, always shouting something or other, laughing and grabbing me a little too hard around the waist. It seemed like nothing could throw him.'

'What happened?'

'Oh, him taking over the bar, mostly. Seamus started spending most of his time on a barstool, with his Exports lying open in front of him and a bottomless whiskey beside. It got so Mick always had a glass in front of him too. Sure, I knew he was a drinker when I married him, but not like that. I remember looking down along the bar at the two of them, my men, mirroring each other like kids, two arms lifting drinks to two sets of lips. I had this fantasy. I'd push

Seamus off his barstool, run the broom along the shelves and send all those bottles crashing to the floor, then grab Mick by the hand and — what? I never got that far. I always just turned around and went home, or back up the stairs to the office. I spent a lot of time up there, playing by myself when I was little, playing with your mother when I was grown up, listening to them laughing through the floorboards. Mick knew I could see through him, and maybe that's why he kept me at arm's length. I kept thinking things would change when Seamus died.'

'Didn't you love each other?'

'We must've, in a way. Maggie, we didn't even sleep in the same room for the last ten years of the marriage. He moved into the guest room one night and neither of us said a word about it. I was livid, though. I'd been dreaming about doing it for ages.'

'But you loved him. You wore mourning for a whole year.'

'It took a while to get used to being on my own.'

'It's not how I remember.'

'From the summers? I'll tell you what I remember. Your father down working in the city and Mick at the Bull. Or out driving God knows where, taking out fenceposts with the nose of our car. Or lying in bed with the curtains drawn, telling me to keep you quiet, to make you play outside.' She takes hold of Maggie's hand. 'You remember him being there, Maggie? Come on. Those summers were the three of us — your mother, you and me.'

'I know, but I thought it was just — work, you know.' Maggie lowers her head. 'I thought you were happy.'

'Well I was, at times. Mick had this pain in him — I never really knew what — but it was like fire, it gave him a kind of glow. A lust for life, that's what I thought it was. And when he turned it my way, I thought it was love.'

The waitress unloads two shakes in stainless steel tumblers, with old-fashioned fountain glasses beside. 'How's the gardening trucker, Else?' She rests her tray on her hip. 'He holding together alright?'

'He's as sane as you or I, Belle.' Elsie peels the paper jacket from her straw. 'You'd best be careful — you'll give credence to the stereotype of the small town gossip.'

'Well, lah-dee-dah.' Belle whirls and sashays away.

Maggie narrows her eyes. 'What'd she mean, *holding it together?*'

'Nothing. Sean was in a bit of a bad way before the crash, that's all, and for a while after. Not crazy though.' She grins. 'Or if he is, then so are we.'

—

In the early morning Sean comes upon a murder of crows, dipping their black beaks into the corn plot, unearthing the kernels they watched him sow. He runs at them, their wings pumping, jumping back to lift away.

On the cottage stoop, he nails two-by-fours into a cross, fills a cloth sack with clippings and ties it on top for a head. In the shed he finds a work shirt and jeans, a straw hat and a pair of stiff gloves. He dresses the stick man, fleshes him out with straw, carries him down to the plot.

—

Maggie leaves the verandah for the afternoon heat. She wanders the vegetable beds — tiny green cherry tomatoes tucked up against stalks, the startling red veins of the chard.

Her eyes follow the side field. The cottage seems small, brown brick under the wings of a tall white spruce. It seems harmless. Inviting even, safe.

At the south window she rests her palms on the brick sill, finding the coarse curtains drawn shut against the sun. She rounds the corner to the back wall, picking a path through wild daisies, then halting, her heart rearing up in her chest.

He crouches over the herb bed on the dappled north side. His back's turned bare — a fraction of his face, his cheek and the shadow of his chin.

She pulls back behind the wall, through the high flowers, not stopping until she's deep into the trees. '*Stupid,*' she hisses, digging nails into the palms of her hands.

Sean feels the weight of a body nearby, movement echoing through the soil beneath his feet. He turns, too late to catch her eyes on his back. Something gentle among the plants. A deer, he thinks.

—

Ed swims through the morphine into the room — it's gotten so Elsie can tell how close he's getting, like watching someone stroking from the far shore of a lake. His eyes fix and focus, jolting her with a surge of joy.

'Rachel?'

The smile falls back down her throat. She remembers the night she asked him why he'd never married.

'Rachel, I want you to see how I've changed — ' His voice falters. 'Elsie?'

She clasps his hand. 'Yes love?'

His eyes move wildly over her face. 'Rachel?'

She takes a deep breath. 'Yes?'

'I didn't do right by you. Didn't love you right.'

'It's alright.' The words present themselves. 'I forgive you.'

He turns his face away, showing his eggshell skull, the runnels of his withering neck. The same skull and neck she stared at, the night he confessed.

'How is it you never married?' She knew it was a silly way to ask — old fashioned and coy — but it was out.

His answer was a while coming. 'I did.'

'Oh. You never mentioned — ' He didn't turn to face her in the bed, as she was hoping he would.

'Her name was Rachel.'

' — Was?'

'I was working in a nickel mine in Sudbury.' He was only sixty then, but his voice came out ancient. 'We were young — I was twenty-two, she was nineteen. She was plump when we met, and as soon as we were married, she started putting on weight. I thought she was pregnant at first. She used to eat twice as much as I could, and fast, stuffing it in like she thought somebody might take it away. I didn't fuss. She was from a big family — I figured she'd never quite gotten her share.' He paused, reaching for a cigarette, lighting it lying down. 'One night she started talking about this hole she had inside, said it was growing, getting bigger no matter what she did. It gave me the creeps the way she was talking — I guess I made some joke and went out on the stoop to smoke. She didn't come to bed that night, just sat up all night in the parlour. After that she didn't come to bed with me again. I saw the doctor and got some pills to help her sleep, but she wouldn't take them, just pushed my hand away. One of the guys at the mine made some crack about my wife getting so fat I'd never get the ring off her finger, and I laughed like a bastard with the rest of them.' He sat up at the edge of the bed, Elsie's hand falling away from his side, lying helpless in front of her on the sheet. 'I started coming home later and later — I'd sit in the bar with the boys, or else go walking the backroads around town. I was eating my suppers at a little place on the highway. The waitress there had arms I could've closed my fingers round — you could see ribs where the uniform stretched out across her back. By then, Rachel wouldn't even look round when I came in. One night, I got home even later than usual. Rachel was in the armchair by the stove. The fire'd burnt out — I could see my breath in front of me, it was that cold. The pill bottle was lying at her feet. I couldn't lift her by myself. I had to get a man from down the road to help me lay her out.'

He hadn't cried to tell the story, but Elsie had, hearing it. They slept not touching, waiting for the heavy ghost that lay between them to fade.

Ed rolls back to her, blinking. 'Rachel? — Elsie?'

'Yes Ed, we're here.'

On the way home from the hospital, Elsie puts her foot to the gas like she's squashing a bug. She sees them as newlyweds. Ed with a full head of hair and a straight back, Rachel veiled, her mouth blooming full through the white.

Elsie had refused to cover her face. Seamus fussed and pleaded, the veil one of the few pieces he kept when the church came for his wife's things, but Elsie held her ground. She planned to recall the whole thing in crisp detail, no net between her and the proceedings. For the same reason, she hardly drank at the reception, though it seemed everyone in town got loaded that night. Sunday-best crowds filing into the Brown Bull, men losing their ties, women slipping stockings off under the rough tables. Seamus sang Danny Boy and cried his heart out, one hand on the piano, holding him upright. Everyone said Mick had enough to down a pack-horse, though he never staggered or slurred a word. He was an engine that night, the alcohol fueling him, driving him on. It was only later, when they were alone together, that she could see how far gone he really was. His huge hands fumbling at his fly, reaching wildly down the front of her dress.

Beside a sunny field, she pulls onto the gravel shoulder, leans across to roll up the passenger window, then settles back and does up her own. Both hands cover her face. She opens her mouth, the wail creeping out slowly, like something locked up too long.

From her bedroom window, Maggie watches him break into the flower bed below. He drives the blade of the shovel into the earth, puts a heel to it and drives it further. He pauses, shifts his weight, then lifts and turns a clod of earth, exposing a snarl of roots.

She imagines him leaning on the shovel to rest, glancing up, catching sight of her where she stands. She backs away, stretching, touching her palms to the glass.

The dream finds the open window, springing up to filter through the flimsy screen. It lands on the table, then leaps to bed, clamping a thin hand over Sean's slack mouth. Water rises in his skull, an ocean of sinking eyes. He thrashes in the sheets, slams his head into the bedpost and wakes.

⟶

Maggie runs a hand over the rosebush, releasing its smell.

'Wild roses mean summer,' Elsie told her once. Maggie was twelve, braids down her back, found sulking among the thickening blooms. The first summer without Katherine — the last summer Maggie spent in Baptiste.

The buds are swelling, sweating a dusky scent. She rolls one in her fingers, feeling it loosen and let go.

Sean closes the door gently. Maggie stands with her back to him, staring into the mess of his unmade bed. Everything seemed simpler outside — he looked up from a bed of violets to find her staring down, stood up and somehow caught hold of her hand.

He shifts on his feet, unsure of what she wants. 'How long are you here for?'

'I don't know.' Silence. Then muttering. 'This is crazy. *Crazy*.' She turns to face him. 'I should go.'

'Don't.' He reaches out and she clutches at his hand, touching it to her lips, guiding it inside her blouse. They stumble to the bed, fumbling with their clothes, collapsing. It's been so long. He can barely hold back, emptying himself into her the moment she cries out.

She reaches for her clothes. He loosens his hold and rolls off. 'What's wrong?'

'Nothing's wrong. I have to go.'

'You have to g-go? Go where?'

She's at the door, face taut, sandals hanging from her hands. 'I have to go,' she says again, and then she's gone.

In choke cherry shadow, Maggie draws her knees close, waiting for her heart to slow.

You should be an actress. For as long as her memory, people telling her, sensing her gift for make-believe.

She faked it. Again.

⬤

Elsie lifts the red and gold cake tin onto her lap and sets the lid aside. She grabs a fistful of photos and passes them to Maggie, one by one.

Mick and Elsie on honeymoon at the coast — him with a silver salmon the length of his arm, her in a spotted kerchief, her young legs bare. 'The man who ran the charter boat took that one.' Elsie laughs. 'Told us to say *sex* instead of *cheese*. That got him in solid with Mick.'

Katherine poses in floor-length taffeta, a sash across her breasts reading, MISS BAPTISTE '69. Her hair teased up high, eyes black and flashing. The boys in the background train their gazes like water on a blaze. 'She looks happy enough,' says Elsie. 'You wouldn't know she was mad as a wet cat.'

Maggie looks up. 'She was? Why?'

'There was a scout in town that day, believe it or not, from one of the modelling agencies in the city. They came out to the rural beauty contests from time to time, still do, I suppose, looking for a diamond in the rough. This one found your mother. He was telling her all about the glamorous life when Mick showed up, all three of his big sheets to the wind. He took that poor man by the collar and nearly shook him to death. *I know your kind! Slithering out from the city to tempt girls with money and stories of the big life! Holding candy out the window of yer car, no better than a buggering perv!* The poor man's face was wet with spit by the time Mick was done with him. Truth be told, I couldn't help feeling just a little proud. Not your mother though — she was livid — wouldn't speak to him for weeks. No one holds a grudge like a sixteen-year-old girl. Oh, he pretended not to care, but she'd never held his drinking against him before that, it was the first time she wouldn't forgive. He was a misery. I woke up more than once to the sound of him slippering down the hall, wearing a track outside Katherine's door. Times like that, I could almost forgive him myself.'

Katherine shows her thin back in the prow of a canoe, head bald under a terry cloth hat, bent forward with chemical fatigue. Maggie lays this one face down on the table.

Elsie cradles a sleeping Maggie across her thighs. The child's fine hair in her fingers, the soft, breathing life in her lap.

'I know these.' Maggie frowns. 'Some of these were Mother's.'

'Your father gave them to me. Didn't he tell you?' Maggie shakes her head. 'He sent me the things he couldn't bear to get rid of and couldn't bear to have around. It's all up in the attic, any time you want to look. Here, this one's a beauty.'

Katherine curls in Bill's lap in the verandah swing, showing her spoken-for hand.

'That ring.' Elsie snorts. 'He had it on installments forever — said he asked for the biggest rock in the place. Lucky thing the place was Goldy's in downtown Baptiste.'

Maggie peers closer. Her father wears his love fiercely, staring at Katherine as though the sight of her causes him pain. 'Jesus,' Maggie whispers, 'you wouldn't know him now. He looks so alive here. So —I don't know — so real.'

'He loved her, Maggie.'

'I know. I know he loved her. You loved her, I loved her, Grandad loved her — but it's like he threw himself in after the coffin.'

Elsie passes the next one in silence. Maggie stands knee-deep in Baptiste Lake, her first bikini not quite flat on her chest, candy-stripe red and white. Her hair hangs in tendrilling strings. She rests her hands on bony hips, her chin unsure.

'Christ,' Maggie mutters.

Elsie draws close. 'That was the last summer.'

'The last day of the last summer. Dad came up to get me, remember? We had that picnic.'

'I remember.' Elsie sighs. 'He was telling me all about the business. Every sentence had zeroes on the end.'

Maggie laughs, the kind of laugh people let out after a car crash. 'You were swimming when he took this.' She points at the photo in her hand, touching her fingertip to the bare belly of her girlish self. 'He held this big beach towel to wrap me in, and I stepped into it, and then he wouldn't let go. He had his face in my hair — it took me a second to figure out he was crying. *You smell like her*, he told me. *You smell like your mother.*'

＞

Maggie knocks lightly on the cottage door, a bold crow muttering behind. Nothing. She knocks again, harder. Nothing. She hammers, then rattles the doorknob, finding it locked.

＞

Sean lifts the brass steer's head and knocks. He's about to knock again when a girl in a white lace apron pulls open the heavy door and nods.

'Hello — '

'He's out by the barns. They're doing the branding. You can go round that way.' She gestures to a chip trail, then closes the door gently in his face.

He follows the smell of singed hide round back of the looming house. Across a corral, two boys lead a cow through the gate, toward the heavy-set man with the iron. A younger man sits smoking on an up-turned bucket. Brand meets flank, the cow bellowing high, then lowing as it's led away. The brander swivels at the sound of Sean's boots. 'Can I help you?'

Sean draws closer, leaning into the fence. 'You Mr Hogarth?'

'I am.'

'I'm Sean Bogue.'

'Well?'

Sean takes a deep breath. 'I was delivering your cattle on the night of the crash. I'm the driver.'

'What?' Hogarth bristles, the iron smoking in his hand. 'You've got a hell of a spine.' The young man eases up from his bucket, eyes dancing between his father and Sean.

'I've come to apologize.'

Hogarth sniffs and spits. 'What's the sense in that? Insurance paid for those that were lost, and you got canned. What else is there?'

'I don't know. I just wanted to tell you I'm sorry. For all those cows that were killed, the calves.'

'Shit.' Hogarth cocks his head. 'I told you, I replaced them.'

'Yeah.' Sean toes a circle in the dirt. 'Well, goodbye.'

Hogarth shakes his head and turns to yell at the two ranch hands. Sean walks away, the sound bouncing off the back of his head. At the truck, the son catches up, flicking his yellow butt into the dust. Sean cuts the engine.

'Wha'd you say your name was?'

'Sean. Sean Bogue.' Sean holds a hand out the window.

'I'm his son.' He reaches out for a single, solid shake. Then looks over his shoulder, back to where his father's marking the herd. 'Glad to know you.' He nods and backs away from the truck.

—

Maggie lies motionless on the floor of her room. She thinks vaguely of standing, but somehow can't — it's like Lilliput — she's held down by a thousand threads. Something scuttles in the corner of her eye. She turns her head. It's huge, drawn up its legs, stacking eight little Maggies in its eyes.

Elsie chases the echoing screams through the house, takes the stairs like a woman half her age.

Later, once Maggie's quiet, she searches the room. 'It's long gone by now — you probably burst it with that scream.' She lifts a T-shirt from the floor. 'You were never scared of spiders, you used to feed that one in the jade plant.'

Maggie drops her face into her hands. 'It was the way it ran for me.'

'What?'

'It ran for me,' she says again, muffled. 'Like it was sent.'

Maggie sleeps, tucked into clean cotton sheets. In the high rafters, a thumbnail spider spins a line and steps off, falling like a feather, touching down on the plain of her forehead. It rests there for a time. Lifting one leg and then another, before rewinding its silk and itself into the height of the room.

In the illusory light of evening, Elsie steps out from the poplars, the dogs bounding before her onto the green. Caley spots it first. She lifts her head and barks, springs forward in a sprint, the pup and Elsie's gaze following her into the sun's red stain. Ed stands in the distance, arms open, feet firm in the soil. Elsie's heart skips. She hurries forward a few steps, until the light shifts slightly and she can see. Caley stops at the plot's edge, drops to her belly and whines. The scarecrow stands faceless over the beginning corn.

The ladder groans under Maggie's bare feet. She reaches up for the trapdoor handle, twisting and pushing into the dark. Her head rises from the silvery floorboards, she flicks on the flashlight and climbs into the stifling room. It's empty, except where the ceiling slants down to three trunks in the dust. She kneels before them, her beam throwing black box shadows into the eaves. Each bears a name, written in bold, indelible ink. *Seamus Hughes. Mick Mahoney. Katherine Mahoney Wolfe.* A box for each of Elsie's dead, like the packages war widows receive in the mail.

She flips the latch of the last trunk and lifts the lid, releasing traces of her mother's perfume. Once, a woman wearing that scent passed her in a downtown mall. Maggie tailed her through several stores, trailing fingers over everything she'd touched.

She reaches into the shadow and draws out a long white veil. She's seen it in pictures — her father in a rented tux, holding the car door open for his bride, her mother stepping out, wild roses in her hands, the veil blowing back from her face.

A heart-shaped stone from the river, *Bill loves Katy*, felt pen outline around her father's bold hand.

A blue velvet ringbox, empty.

A silver frame, Katherine beaming, newborn Maggie at her breast.

Then a letter. *To Miss Katherine Mahoney*, again, her father's script, pressed hard into delicate paper. She hesitates for a moment, before digging under the envelope's lip.

> *Dear Katherine,*
>
> *Ever since the night of the dance, I have thought of nothing but you. Did you know I left my friends to hitch back to Nestow when I drove you home? I'm not very popular with them right now. No skin off my back, I'll be leaving them behind when I go to the college in fall. Anyway, I'm writing to tell you I'll be in Baptiste with my father for the livestock auction in a few weeks time. I plan to come see you.*
>
> *Yours truly,*
> *Bill Wolfe*
>
> *P.S. You were like a piece of fire on the dance floor in that red dress.*

Maggie follows his words, holding her breath, then drawing and holding it again. The lines blur. She folds the letter and slips it back.

Last is a pillowy plastic bag. She draws out the shawl, crocheted lambswool, velvety black. Katherine wore it every evening, reading in the big red chair. A gift from Elsie, one birthday before the bad time came.

She finds Elsie dozing in the wicker swing. 'Gran? Can I keep this?''

Elsie pales a little as she leans out to take the shawl from Maggie's shoulders. She holds it at arms length, then draws it to her face, clasping it over her nose like a child.

Maggie shifts on her feet. 'You don't want me to.'

'No,' Elsie says quietly. Then thrusts the black bundle into Maggie's arms. 'Take it.'

—

Sean draws the door open quickly, like someone trying to catch sight of a ghost. Maggie says nothing, just stands with her arms at her sides until he pulls her in. Their mouths meet — open — they drop to their knees on the rough wool rug.

She's promised herself, but it's as if she has no choice — he moans quietly and she panics, forcing sounds of release from her throat. He lets himself go, straining, then relaxing against her. She counts ten. Then reaches out from under him for her blouse.

'What's the hurry?' Anger in his voice. Or hurt.

She fumbles with the buttons.

'Maggie.' He stops her hand. 'I want you to stay.' She looks up at him through her hair. 'What is it?'

She stands and steps into her shorts. 'Nothing. I have to go.'

'Stay.'

'Stay?' She whirls at the door. 'I'm not your fucking dog.'

'What?' He shrinks back as though slapped. 'C-christ.' His face hardens. She opens her mouth as though to speak, then shuts it, and the door behind her.

—

Maggie feels along the edge of the shawl, following the gentle scallops as though she were blind. Her fingers stumble on a lump — the spot where Elsie drew the last loop tight and wove it in. It begins innocently enough, fiddling a little, then picking, as though it were something she'd found on her skin. A black tail appears. Two sharp tugs and the wool lets loose, unravelling for several yards before it snags. Her breath coming shallow and fast. She curls down over the darkness in her lap, prying viciously, feeling it give and slip away through her hands.

———

Deep down the back of the property, Sean stumbles on a fallen birch, lying like a long white torso in a flowering raspberry briar. He climbs the tangle of disinterred roots and swings up onto the trunk, walking toward the branches, a sea of cat's-eye leaves.

As a boy, he climbed hundreds of trees. Whenever they moved to a new base, he scouted for low branches, bowed trunks or uneven bark. One summer in Comox, he lost his grip in the first high limbs of a pine. He didn't know enough to let go and fall free, bending his knees to land. He held close to the tree the whole way down — the shirt pushing up around his neck, bark skinning his chest, his arms, the insides of his bony knees. He ran home howling, the salt wind whipping his flesh. At the doorstep he met a tall uniform, face shaded under the brim of a Lieutenant's hat. 'Daddy,' he whimpered, for the first and last time. His mother came running. His father stepped round him and strode away stiff to the car.

Sean crouches into the crook of a branch. Stillness and heat, his eyes dragging as he sags into the leaves. Then a cry, otherworldly, silver wings falling down from the sky.

The goshawk lands at the foot of the birch, a freshly-killed starling in its grasp. Blood darkens the bark, the starling framed, twisted neck, glinting feathers and broken-twig feet. The hawk balances. Begins to knead, to rock — head cocked and metallic breast — it rocks on the fine bow of the starling's back.

Then stops, dead still, fixing both its red eyes on Sean.

Slowly, delicately, it lifts a clawed foot. Holds it out to him, beseechingly, like a hand.

Twisted in sheets, in deepest night, Maggie comes upon her mother. Katherine's frail under a grey blanket, hands folded like the skeletons of birds. She lifts one and beckons, hooking Maggie from the far side of the room. 'It's here.' She tucks Maggie's hand under the blanket, holding it over her swollen womb. 'You understand?' Her grip tightens.

'Mother, please — ' Maggie struggles, but Katherine's strong. She drags Maggie's fingers down through remnants of hair, resting them in dry, fleshy folds. 'Here,' she whispers, then lets go, the bed empty where she lay.

Half-awake, Maggie runs a hand through her hair, combing the dream away. She feels across her belly, pressing for pain, probing for possible lumps. A familiar ache. She eases the sheet down to find blood, wet beneath her, dark on the white of her thigh.

Maggie stands at the back door, watching him clear a dead section of hedge, his bare arm guiding a gas-powered saw. He draws the back of his gloved hand across his forehead, a simple gesture that somehow makes her decide. She throws open the door, takes the old steps two at a time.

'Sean — ' she says, 'Sean!' but he's deaf with earplugs and the muffled whine of the saw. She hesitates, then lays a hand on his shoulder, the touch from nowhere making him whirl. He cuts the motor, plucks the foam cylinders from his ears.

'Sorry — ' He holds up a hand and she lowers her voice. 'Sorry I startled you.'

He shrugs, his body wooden, like a fort.

'I've got something to tell you.'

He nods, his lips pressed together.

'I've been lying to you.'

'Christ Maggie, just tell me and get it over.'

'I'm trying. I've never — come. During sex. Had an orgasm.'

'What?'

His face frightens her. 'I started faking from my first time. I've gotten used to it. Up until you I didn't think about it much — ' the words die down under his stare. 'Oh shit. Forget it.' She turns to go.

He pulls her round, his mouth on hers, sudden and bewildering. When they come apart, he keeps a firm hold on her shoulders and speaks gently. 'I thought you were going to say you were leaving — maybe you had someone back in Toronto.'

'What? No. I had someone — lots of someones, actually.' She looks down on a red ladybug, climbing the bridge of her foot. 'I don't want to pretend with you.'

He watches her go, lifting hips, calves shifting through the brilliant grass. The saw starts effortlessly, rising weightless in his hand.

'There was a call for you.' Elsie watches Maggie's face fall over an armful of wild flowers.

' — Oh?'

'Somebody called Steven.'

'Stephane? Actually you're right, it's Steven on his birth certificate.'

'Steven, Stephane. He said to tell you you're in breach of contract and he wants your shit out of his place.' She imitates Stephane's Queen Street drawl. 'Who is he?'

Maggie drops her bouquet on the table and collapses into a chair. 'He's the bastard I've been wasting my time with for the past year.' She groans. 'He's a hot shit director, he's my boss in a way — I guess I should say *was*. I'd heard the stories about him, but I managed to forget them when he asked me out.' She shakes her head. 'Everything — moved around him. I can't explain it. The world got so small.' She fingers a columbine spur. 'The night before I came here, we went to this big art opening. I lost track of him fairly early on, kept myself busy getting way too drunk. I found him bent over some woman. You'd think he could've found a room with a lock on the door.' She falls silent, rubbing small circles into her temples.

Elsie tucks her chair in close to the table. 'I found Mick with a woman once.'

Maggie looks up, the words like something falling, smashing open on the floor.

'She was the wife of one of the railroad workers, Mrs Fisher — Loretta or Roxanne, one of those kind of names. I used to see her at the school when I picked up your mother. Bleached-out hair and watery eyes, always teetering on a pair of heels. I'd heard she was always leaving her kids alone to go down to the Bull after her husband.' Elsie draws a deep breath. 'One night when Katherine was at a sleep-over, I got dressed around midnight and drove down to the bar. It was an impulse — I thought maybe we'd take a walk along the river like we used to. The place was empty. I took the steps down to the cellar — I figured he'd be down there, getting up stock. He was there alright. I swung the door open to find him going at her on the concrete floor.'

'Jesus. What did you say?'

'Say? Nothing. Nothing to say. He jumped off. I walked back up the stairs with him following, stuffing it back in his pants. She pushed past us at the door and stumbled away down the street. I suppose she went home to find her husband dead drunk in their bed. Neither one of us spoke on the way home. I drove fast, took the bends in the road a little wide. At the door I told him never to let me catch him at it again. Strange that I put it like that, don't you think?'

'Did he ever?'

'I think so. I smelled her on him, her or someone else who hosed herself down with dime store cologne. Never caught him at it again, though. Never walked down by the river with him again either.'

⁓

'Where's Maggie?' Sean stands looking up the verandah steps.

Elsie lays her book aside. 'I'm afraid I put her on the early bus.'

'What? Why didn't she — shit.'

Elsie hides her smile. 'Those ribs of yours pretty much good as new?'

'Huh? Oh, yeah.' He fingers the left side of his chest.

'Come for supper this evening. We'll keep each other company.'

Tools slip from his fingers. He crouches in the flowerbeds, strangling the dandelions, ripping chickweed like fistfuls of hair.

Elsie stuffs a chicken with wild rice and slides it into the oven. Limps out to the vegetable patch to fill her apron with tender leaves.

When Sean arrives in a clean white shirt, she takes his hand and leads him to the dining room table. 'Sit.' She disappears into the kitchen.

'Can I help?'

She backs in through the swinging door and sets the chicken down. 'You can carve.' She points to an oversize knife and fork, the antler-handled set Mick gave her one Christmas, won in a raffle at the Elks.

She returns with a bright salad and hoots at the mess he's making of the bird. 'Didn't anyone ever show you how?' She repositions his hands.

'I guess not.' He slices carefully, flesh falling away under the blade. 'My father wasn't really one to share things.'

'Yep.' She pulls out her chair. 'I taught myself after Mick died.'

'White or dark?'

'I like a bit of both.'

He lays meat on her plate, drumstick and a slice of breast. 'How long have you lived here, Mrs Mahoney?'

'You want me to start calling you Mr Bogue?'

'Hell no.'

'Well then. I've lived here from the moment I was born.'

'I can't imagine that. You like it?'

'I do now. Not always though. There've been times when I was ready to burn this house to the ground.' She pushes the salad bowl his way. 'It was good when Mick and I were new. In the summers too, when Katherine came up from the city with Maggie in tow.' She smiles slyly. 'It's been best for the past six years.'

He looks up from his plate.

'You've never asked about the man who used to do your job. You must've wondered.'

'Maggie said he was sick. I didn't — '

'More than sick. Dying.'

'Oh.'

'You never know what life has up its sleeve. I thought I was finished with men when Mick died, I really did. Then old Ed strolled up from that cottage and laid his heart on my steps.'

'Wow.'

'Wow is right.'

Sean swallows. 'Elsie, in the hospital, that first time, you said — '

'I said I'd almost driven into the river.'

'Yeah.'

'And I said I'd tell you all about it. Well, I was lonely. That's the thing about living with drunks — Mick was always at the bar, and Seamus before him, the two of them their own best customers. It was one of the nights when Mick didn't make it home — maybe passed out at the Bull, or else drinking straight through, maybe in some other woman's bed — it didn't seem to matter which. The fact was, my marriage was dead. My marriage was dead, my daughter was dead, and I was getting old in an empty bed. I decided to get up and poach myself an egg — it sounds silly, but that's what Seamus gave me when I couldn't sleep, said it put the eye of God in your belly. Anyway, I wasn't paying attention. I had the water boiling way too hard. The egg went all wrong when I dropped it in, turned inside-out and started growing those nasty little tails. It upset me, made me frantic somehow, the way it was jumping around in the pot. I grabbed the car keys and then I was driving — still in my nightie, if you please — driving so fast I passed my turn-off in the dark and had to double back. It wasn't a road so much as a couple old dirt tracks. Lead right up to the river, one of those spots where the water narrows and runs hard, down deep into holes it's been digging since the riverbed began. Davy-Jones's lockerettes, Seamus called them, sinkholes where the river sucks you down. He took me fishing there once, told me how whole rafts of men'd gone down there in olden times. Anyway, I was parked up the bank a bit, staring out the windshield, picturing those men in their buckskin, tilting and slipping away. I don't know how exactly, but somewhere in there, I just shifted into gear and brought my foot down hard on the gas.' She touches her knife to her lips. 'It was the river itself that stopped me, all that water breaking white under the moon. I stomped on the brake with about half a second to spare.' She chuckles. 'Took a while to back out of there — I had to strip branches and build them up under the wheels. That pot had boiled dry by the time I got home, and the egg burnt away to nothing.' She wrinkles her nose. 'The stink of it! I opened every damn window and door, even upstairs, where the smoke hadn't gotten so bad. Then I brewed myself a strong cup of tea. Sat down and drank it, feeling the wind blow through my house.'

Sean sits forward in his chair. 'I think it was the same — for me, I mean.'

She holds up her glass. 'Clever lad.'

Maggie looks out on Spadina and Queen though the streetcar window. Girls bend greedy, running hands over a vendor's glittering cart. Pony-tailed men swing portfolios. A drug-skinny punk hauls back hard on his dog's choker chain.

There's not a soul, she realizes suddenly, not a single soul she wants to call while she's in town.

The malamute drops a small black ball at Elsie's feet. She kicks with the tip of her toe, sending the ball bouncing to the far end of the verandah, the pup bounding after. She runs her fingers through the setter's silky hair, strokes the long red chin that lies across her lap. That morning Ed came to just long enough to ask after the dogs — was she walking them enough, making sure they got in a good run. She was furious. 'Come home and walk them yourself if you're so worried,' she blurted. Then buried her face in her hands.

Maggie finds her belongings piled like a pyre in a corner of Stephane's sky-lit space. Balanced on top, the perfume he gave her on her birthday. Burnt violets with an undertone of meat. She'd rubbed it into her neck for him, her wrists, even between her thighs.

She climbs to the bed loft, empties what's left of it into his slippery sheets.

Elsie finds Sean in the vegetable patch, caging the tomatoes for support. 'Hey loverboy, she's coming into Edmonton tomorrow. Said for me to give you the flight number and time.' She holds out a slip of paper.

He stands slowly and opens his hand. Shuts his eyes, as though waiting to be caned.

Maggie looks out from the wings, as two young women circle each other on stage, snarling and baring their teeth. Stephane gleams in the front row, draped like a stole on his seat.

'Feral!' He yells suddenly, stopping the women in their tracks. 'You're actors aren't you? Give me feral!'

Maggie laughs out loud. Steps out from stage left in her new white dress. 'Hi Steve.'

His mouth puckers like a cut. 'Well, well. You look — different.'

'You mean healthy?'

'Sure, if that's what you need to believe. You out of my place?'

'Yep.' She tosses him her keys. 'Where's my cheque?'

'You're lucky to be getting one.'

She narrows her eyes. 'Where is it?'

' — Lee has it upstairs.' He smiles. 'Seen the reviews? I guess you thought you couldn't be replaced.'

'I saw you replace me, remember?' She gathers her hem in her hand, crouches at the edge of the stage and leaps down.

He shrinks back a little. 'I'm talking about the show.'

She's already past him. Striding up the aisle, the dress billowing out white in her wake.

On the way to the hospital, Elsie pulls over by a field of wild daisies.

Ed never did a thing for the patch out back of the cottage, just planted the first few and watched them go forth and multiply. 'I like that,' he told her once. 'A flower that grows up straight and strong, with nobody to watch over it but the sky.'

She climbs the shallow ditch and wades into the field, stooping down to snap stems close to the base. Their smell, more animal than flower, so raw her eyes begin to run.

She stands beside his bed, arranging the yellow-eyed flowers in a vase.

'Elsie? That you?' His voice high as child's now, barely any flesh left to weigh it down.

'It's me, love.' She kisses him, mouth open, tasting death.

Sean spots Maggie first through the welcoming crowd, circles round and grabs her, making her scream.

Back at the truck, three wild roses lie on her seat. He clears his throat and speaks slowly. 'See that? One for every night you were away.'

—

Elsie stands a split second before the phone rings, the spine watery in her back.

'Mrs Mahoney?'

'Oh God.'

'I'm afraid he's gone.'

She holds out a hand to find the wall.

'Mrs Mahoney?'

'I'll be right there.'

She takes the steps too fast, feels her hip buckle and give way, dropping her in a heap on the ground. Dirt in her mouth. Nothing fractured. She wouldn't be hauling herself up like this. She wouldn't be walking, however slow and lopsided, to her car.

—

The service is crowded and short, casket closed, Ed being a private man. Most of the town follows to the plot, standing back while gravediggers begin filling the hole. Elsie sends Sean to the truck for the daisy clump she dug up from behind the cottage. She shovels down beside the headstone. Lowers the roots into their new home, pulling earth in around them, patting it firm.

Maggie helps Elsie up the long staircase to her room, turns down the covers and eases her into bed. Beneath them, Sean searches the kitchen cupboards, boils water and warms the pot. He carries the tea up on a tray, stoops to lay it down at the door. 'I'll sleep downstairs on the couch. Call if you need me.'

Maggie looks round. 'You don't have to — '

'Of course I do.'

She listens to his footfalls on the stairs, then turns to find her grandmother fast asleep. Elsie's head rests lightly on the pillow, as though she were floating, buoyant in the sea of her grief.

The dream finds him, mouth open, arm dangling from the couch. He hovers for a moment, then draws into himself and dives, swimming deep into a human school. He feels the water grow calm. Feels the bottom rise up to meet him, like a sun.